Wishbone and Joe followed
Mr. King down the block
to the bank.

When Mr. King went inside, Wishbone and Joe kept an eye on him from the bank's window.

After waiting in line, Mr. King went to one of the teller windows. He signed a form. Then the teller handed him a stack of paper bills. Mr. King pulled an envelope out of his suit jacket and placed the bills inside.

"That's interesting," Joe said to himself. "Why did he put the money in an envelope instead of in his wallet?"

"That's terribly interesting," Wishbone told Joe. "Wait a second. *Why* is that so interesting?"

Joe put a hand to his head, as if making a big discovery. "Maybe he put the money in an envelope because he doesn't plan to keep it. Could it be *bribe money* that he's planning to give to the surveyors working in the park?"

"Yes. That *must* be it!" Wishbone said, his tongue panting with excitement. "He's planning to pay them off so they'll say exactly what he wants them to say about the land measurements. Then he'll be able to build that Tastee Oasis wherever he wants!"

Books in The Adventures of WISHBONE™ series:

Books in The Super Adventures of WISHBONE™ series:

*coming soon

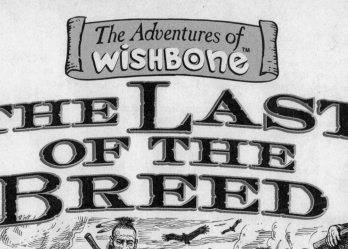

The Adventures of WISHBONE™

THE LAST OF THE BREED

by Alexander Steele

Inspired by *The Last of the Mohicans*
by James Fenimore Cooper
WISHBONE™ created by Rick Duffield

Big Red Chair Books™, *A Division of Lyrick Publishing*™

This book is a work of fiction. The characters, incidents, and dialogues are products of the author's imagination and are not to be construed as real. Any resemblance to actual events or persons, living or dead, is entirely coincidental.

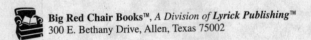 **Big Red Chair Books**™, *A Division of* **Lyrick Publishing**™
300 E. Bethany Drive, Allen, Texas 75002

©1999 Big Feats! Entertainment

Edited by Kevin Ryan

Copy edited by Jonathon Brodman

Cover design by Lyle Miller

Interior illustrations by Don Punchatz

Wishbone photograph by Carol Kaelson

Library of Congress Catalog Card Number: 98-86181

ISBN: 1-57064-273-7

First printing: January 1999

10 9 8 7 6 5 4 3 2 1

Printed in the United States of America

To all the Native Americans
who continue to live

FROM THE BIG RED CHAIR . . .

Oh . . . hi! Wishbone here. You caught me right in the middle of some of my favorite things—books. Let me welcome you to THE ADVENTURES OF WISHBONE. In each of these books, I have adventures with my friends in Oakdale and imagine myself as a character in one of the greatest stories of all time. This story takes place in the summer, when Joe is twelve, and he and his friends are about to enter the sixth grade—during the first season of my television show.

In **THE LAST OF THE BREED**, I imagine I'm Hawkeye, a sharp-shooting woodsman from James Fenimore Cooper's classic tale **THE LAST OF THE MOHICANS**. It's an exciting story about the survival and adventures of a group of travelers during the French and Indian War.

You're in for a a real treat, so pull up a chair and a snack and sink your teeth into **THE LAST OF THE BREED!**

Chapter One

Wishbone ran through the magnificent greenery of Jackson Park. As the trees flew by, the grassy earth felt tender and rich beneath the dog's rapidly pounding paws.

Wow! *Things could not be going any better,* the white-with-brown-and-black-spots Jack Russell terrier thought. *I'm running free in nature, it's a wonderfully sunny day, and it's summer. That means my friends have nothing else to do but play with me!*

Wishbone stopped to say hello to a noble old oak tree. "How are you, Mr. Oak?" Wishbone said as he sniffed around the trunk. "Ah, you're smelling mighty fine this morning. It must be because of that long rain shower the other night. Let's see, do I need to . . . No, I guess not. Well, I'll see you later. I'd better go check on my friends."

Wishbone spun around and raced toward three kids who were walking through the park.

"Are you having fun, boy?" Joe Talbot called to the dog.

Joe was a good-natured twelve-year-old boy whose chief markings were straight brown hair and a great smile. There was no one braver, or better on the basketball court, than Joe. Wishbone lived with Joe and considered the boy his very best buddy.

"Yes, I'm having fun," Wishbone told Joe. "How about throwing a stick for me to chase?"

"I think he's just as happy as we are to be out on a great summer day," Samantha Kepler said with a laugh.

Sam was a kind girl. Her markings were green eyes and silky blond hair, which was pulled back into a ponytail. She was tops when it came to doing anything that was artistic.

"Yes, I'm happy about the summer day," Wishbone told Sam. "Now, how about throwing a stick for me to chase?"

"It almost looks as if he's smiling," David Barnes observed. His markings were dark, curly hair and curious eyes. David was a whiz at doing anything related to science or computers.

Joe, Sam, and David spent so much time with Wishbone that the dog counted them as members of his pack.

"Yes, I'm smiling," Wishbone told David. "Now, what about throwing that stick? And, tell me, why is it that no one around here ever listens to the dog? Am I speaking a foreign language or something?"

Joe picked up a stick from the ground. "Here, boy, you want to go chase a stick?"

"Oh, that sounds like an excellent idea," Wishbone remarked. "Finally, someone listened."

8

As Joe pulled back his arm to throw the stick, Wishbone raced forward. While running at full speed, the dog looked back to watch the stick sail through the cloudless blue sky. When the stick began to angle downward, Wishbone pushed his paws against the ground and then sprang high into the air. With perfect timing, he caught the stick firmly between his canine teeth. After he landed, Wishbone gave himself a tail wag of congratulations.

"Nice catch, Wishbone," a familiar voice said.

Wishbone turned to see Dan Bloodgood, one of the local mail carriers, sitting on a nearby bench. He was a solidly built man with longish black hair and had a wise way about him. Wishbone knew dogs often didn't get along with mail carriers, but he considered Mr. Bloodgood one of his favorite people in Oakdale.

Wishbone dropped the stick and stood on his hind legs. "Good to see you, Dan. Say, how about a treat?"

Mr. Bloodgood smiled. He seemed to understand

Wishbone's words better than most folks did. Wishbone always wondered if this had something to do with the fact that Mr. Bloodgood was a Native American. Wishbone knew many Native Americans had a special relationship with animals.

"So you want one of these, huh?" Mr. Bloodgood said. He reached into his mail cart and pulled out a meat-flavored doggie treat. In addition to delivering the mail to the people, Mr. Bloodgood also delivered his special treats to all the dogs. For this reason, Wishbone thought Mr. Bloodgood had one of the most important jobs in Oakdale.

By the time Wishbone gobbled up the treat, Joe, Sam, and David had come over. "Hi, Mr. Bloodgood," Joe said with a wave. "How's it going?"

Sadness seemed to cloud the mail carrier's face. "Oh, things have been better."

"What's the matter?" Sam asked, taking a seat beside Mr. Bloodgood.

"Mr. Leon King is planning to build a Tastee Oasis fast-food restaurant on the northeastern edge of Jackson Park."

"He can't," David said, plopping onto the ground. "He already tried to build one on the land just east of the park. But so many people in town protested that we stopped him."

Wishbone knew all about this last matter. Leon King was a local real estate developer with a heart made of money. A few months ago, he had tried to build a Tastee Oasis on some land alongside the park. But Joe, Sam, David, and a large group of other locals protested to the town council, and the council had decided not to let Mr. King build on the land.

"This time Mr. King might get his way," Mr. Bloodgood told the others. "A few months ago, he was planning to develop land that he had bought from the town. It was easy enough for the town leaders to change their minds. But this time, Mr. King bought the land he's planning to develop from a private company. That means the town doesn't really have the power to stop him."

"How do you know about this?" David asked.

"There are some men over there surveying the land," Mr. Bloodgood said, pointing in the distance. "I spoke with them a few minutes ago."

Wishbone followed the direction of Mr. Bloodgood's finger. Through some trees, he saw two men wearing work clothes. One of the men held a clipboard; the other one was looking through an instrument that stood on a tripod.

Joe looked upset. "Those guys are surveying land right inside the park! The park belongs to the town! How could Mr. King have bought that land from a private company?"

"According to Mr. King," Mr. Bloodgood said with a shrug, "that land right there isn't part of the park."

"Well, here we go again," Wishbone said. "When it comes to this Tastee Oasis deal, Mr. King is like a dog refusing to let go of a bone."

"I bet Mr. King has some kind of trick up his sleeve," Sam told Mr. Bloodgood. "A few months ago when he tried to build a Tastee Oasis, before the town was planning to sell that land to Mr. King, local workers put up a bunch of signs on the property. Those signs announced a town council hearing so citizens could discuss the sale. But somebody knocked down most of the signs—on purpose, I suspect. We're pretty sure it was Mr. King. He didn't want anyone not in favor of his plan at that town council hearing. Luckily, a big enough group of us spoke out in front of the town council before it was too late."

"I don't trust him," Joe said with a frown. "Mr. Leon King will stop at nothing to make money."

Wishbone dug impatiently at the ground with his front paws. "Yeah. This guy is sneakier than three cats put together."

"Well, it seems the town doesn't trust him, either," Mr. Bloodgood added. "Those men over there don't work for Mr. King. They were hired by the town. They're checking to see if King's measurements really match up with what's on the land deed."

David looked over at the workers. "There's no way that land isn't part of the park. There's just no way!"

"You know," Mr. Bloodgood said, letting his eyes wander over the park's greenery, "my ancestors didn't believe land should be owned at all—not by anyone. When the first European settlers came to this country, the Native Americans welcomed them. They were quite willing to share this country with anyone. But the settlers felt the need to own the land. They kept fighting until they owned almost every inch of it."

"Those settlers didn't treat the Native Americans

very well," Sam said. "They didn't even refer to them by a correct name. When Columbus first arrived here, he thought he had landed in India. He called the people he saw in this part of the world 'Indians.'"

David rubbed his lower lip in thought. "We can't do anything about Columbus or the early settlers. But I wish there was something we could do about Jackson Park. A Tastee Oasis would ruin the natural scenery around here."

"I'm really upset by the idea," Mr. Bloodgood said with a sigh. "I come to this part of the park every day on my mid-morning break. I treasure my time here among the trees and grass and birds and all the other living things."

"Me, too," Wishbone said. He watched a squirrel streak up the side of a tree. "But sometimes those squirrels get on my nerves. And once I caught a few of them throwing acorns at me."

A warm breeze blew through the branches, carrying many scents to Wishbone's nose. The dog's ears picked up the carefree sounds of children playing in different parts of the park. Wishbone loved the park. He disliked the idea that he might lose even the smallest piece of it to a greedy real estate developer.

Joe dug a heel into the ground. "If Mr. King does have a trick up his sleeve, maybe we can figure out what it is. Then we can try to stop him again."

"If there is a trick," Mr. Bloodgood said as he got off the bench, "somebody had better find out what it is—and soon. It's already ten o'clock. As soon as these guys over there are done with their work, they'll take their findings to the town officials. If everything checks out, the mayor and town council will give Mr. King the final okay to build. He's supposed to meet with them at noon. I'd look into this myself if I could, but I have to get back to my mail route."

Wishbone began to run around in an excited circle. "Come on, everyone. We can dig into this. We need to keep the park the way it is. It's the perfect mission for us!"

"Why don't the three of us look into this?" Sam said, springing to her feet. "We might be able to come up with something in the next two hours."

"Uh . . . Sam, make that the *four* of us. Come on," Wishbone said as he began to run away. "Let's get going. No time to waste!"

"But what are we going to do?" David asked, as he got off the ground.

"Oh, right," Wishbone said, running back to his friends. "Good question. What are we going to do?"

"Why don't we find Mr. King and ask him about the deal? He might accidentally give us some kind of tipoff to what he has in mind," Sam said.

"Good idea," Joe said with a determined nod.

"Speaking to Mr. King would not hurt," Mr. Bloodgood said. "I'll meet all of you in front of the town hall at a quarter to twelve. If you find out something, we'll tell the mayor and town council about it. If you don't find out anything, we can at least speak our mind on the subject.

"Okay, gang, follow me," Wishbone called as he scampered ahead. "We've got ourselves a park to save!"

You know, this whole situation reminds me of an old story. It's a tale about Native Americans who depended on the land for survival, and about how certain white people fought to seize the land so they could civilize it their way.

The story was written in 1826 by James Fenimore Cooper. He was one of the very first well-known American authors. This story was one of the first books to describe the landscape and give a feeling for the American wilderness.

Ah, yes, just thinking about this book, I can smell the scented evergreens of the forest and hear the piercing cry of the Indian war whoop. I'm referring, of course, to that most exciting of novels, *The Last of the Mohicans!*

Chapter Two

Wishbone journeyed deep into his imagination. He pictured himself as Hawkeye, a backwoodsman who lived in the North American wilderness in the middle of the 1700s. He was an honest man with a kindly heart. If he was forced to fight, however, there was no one fiercer.

Late on a lazy July afternoon in the year 1757, two men were relaxing beside a stream. For a long time neither man spoke. They simply sat, watching the water flow gracefully over the rocks.

The one known as Hawkeye lay down. His furred belly rested against the earth. He wore a shirt the color of the forest so he would not be seen easily. This shirt was called a hunting shirt and was decorated with beads. Hawkeye also wore a pair of leggings and a cap with a feather—all made of animal skin. Except for a few brown and black spots, his fur was bleached a

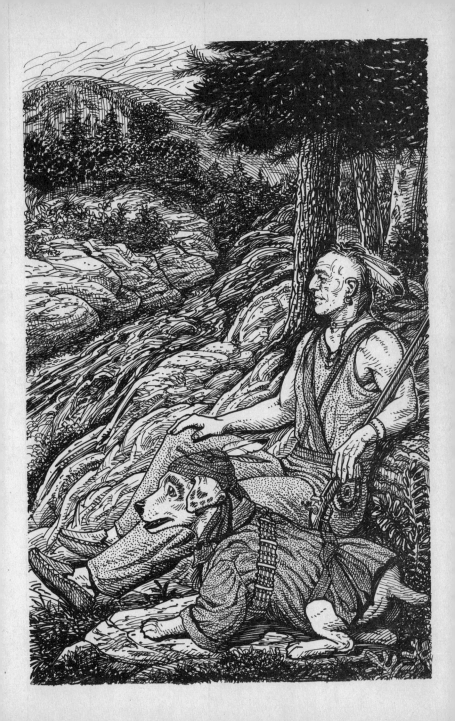

bright white from his many hours spent in the sun. His paws were toughened from their thousands of miles of hiking and tracking of animals. His face showed the ruggedness of a person who had bared his teeth against many deadly dangers.

Hawkeye had spent most of his forty years living off the land. He had no wife, which may have been because he considered nature his true sweetheart. He had no regular job, either. Occasionally, he served as a scout to people who traveled through the thick woods and needed an experienced guide. Though he was a white man, Hawkeye's four strong legs could tread through the forest as well as those of any Indian or animal.

Back in those days, the terms "Indian" and "red man" were used. Nowadays, it's more correct and respectful to use the term "Native American." Some people like to say "American Indian."

The man next to Hawkeye rested his back against a moss-covered log. He was Chingachgook, an Indian of about Hawkeye's own age. In the lines around his eyes and mouth, one could see a sense of dignity, wisdom, and bravery.

The Indian's head was shaved bald, except for a section of black hair on top. A single eagle's feather was tied there. This way of wearing the hair was common for Indian warriors in the northeastern part of what is now the United States.

Chingachgook's bronzed body was covered by a sleeveless hunting shirt, a pair of leggings, and two pieces of material that hung from his waist in front

18

and back—a garment known as a "breechcloth." On his feet he wore moccasins. Like Hawkeye, he wore clothing that was also made of animal skin.

Hawkeye and Chingachgook were surrounded by forest, far away from town or settlement. So many trees grew in the area that they created a leafy green ceiling that revealed only a few scattered patches of sky. It was a shady and sheltered world, filled with many mysteries. The leaves seemed to whisper endless secrets. Hundreds of animal creatures lived nearby, completely unseen. Soft beams of sunlight slanted through the trees, as if filtering their way through the stained glass of a cathedral.

"Is not this a wondrous day?" Hawkeye said in the Indian's native language.

"Yes," Chingachgook replied. "Soon it will darken into a wondrous night."

Hawkeye let his eyes roam through the trees. He admired how each one had a shape and character all its own. The scout's floppy ears were extremely alert. Somewhere far away he picked up the steady tap-tap-tap of a woodpecker.

"I know we are sitting somewhere in the British colony of New York," Hawkeye mentioned. "But to me it looks just like a bunch of nice scenery. You know what, friend? I'm thirsty."

Hawkeye walked over to the stream. After lowering his muzzle, he lapped up the crystal-clear water with the tip of his tongue. Feeling refreshed, he then returned to his spot beside Chingachgook.

After a time, Chingachgook spoke. "When I went

on that last journey alone, I discovered something. Now I must tell it to you."

"I'm all ears," Hawkeye said. He raised his ears to their full height.

"Here the stream is very narrow," Chingachgook said, staring at the flowing water. "But as it flows downward, it meets the big river that then flows into the giant ocean. If that water flowed backward, it would be like my people—the people of the Mohican tribe."

Hawkeye tilted his head with confusion. "I'm afraid I don't follow your meaning."

"Before the white men came to this land," Chingachgook explained, "my people were great in number, like the waters of the ocean. The waters gave us their fish, the woods gave us their deer, and the air gave us its birds. We took loving wives who gave us beautiful children. We were happy and passed on our deep appreciation to God, the Great Spirit. Then the white men came to these shores. They brought disease and trickery . . . and war."

"I will not deny it," Hawkeye said. He scratched his side with his back paw. "I'm a white man myself. But, I confess, my people have many ways of which I do not approve. I surely do not like this ugly war that's going on right now."

Let's take a time-out for a brief history lesson. The war Hawkeye mentions is the French and In-dian War. It took place from 1754 to 1763. The name is misleading. The war was actually fought between the French and the British. Both of these

European countries wanted to control the entire northeastern part of North America.

All of this land had been the home of many different Native American tribes. A lot of Native Americans did get involved in the war. Some tribes fought alongside the French military forces, while other tribes fought alongside the British.

The fact was, neither France nor Britain nor any Native American tribe would end up with this land. The Revolutionary War took place a few years later. After that, most of the land became part of the United States of America. Okay, back to the story.

"Because of the white man's wars and ways," Chingachgook continued, "my people have shrunk in number until we are as narrow as this stream. On my last journey, I learned there are no more of my tribe. My son and I are the only two survivors in whose veins flows the pure blood of the Mohicans. When we leave the earth, our race will live no longer."

Hawkeye dug a paw at the ground. That was something he did whenever he thought about a matter of great importance. Finally, he said, "Such knowledge brings me a deep sadness, Chingachgook. A deep sad——"

Suddenly the scout whipped his muzzle around. He sensed someone behind him. He saw a young Indian standing there. "Ach, man!" Hawkeye shouted. "You sneak up on a fellow quieter than a lizard!"

Hawkeye was only pretending to be angry. The young man was his other best friend, Uncas, Chingachgook's son. His clothing and hair were similar to his father's, as were the features of his face. There was a youthful pride and energy about Uncas that made it seem he could go anywhere and conquer anything. His bronzed body was in perfect condition.

"I bring us food," Uncas said. He pointed to a dead deer that he had just laid down and stretched out on the ground nearby.

"It is a big one," Hawkeye said, licking his chops. "That will make us plenty of fine meals."

"I had to shoot a big one," Uncas said with a wide smile. "You have hunger of a man ten times your size."

Chingachgook pointed at Hawkeye and laughed. The two Mohicans frequently joked with Hawkeye about his large appetite. Then all three men fell silent before murmuring a prayer to the dead deer.

Hawkeye and his Mohican friends often hunted animals. They did so, however, only when they needed the meat for food, or the skins for some purpose, like making clothing. Even then, the men had great respect for the animals they killed. They never failed to thank the creatures for the necessary gifts they provided.

When the three companions finished their prayer, Uncas lay flat on the ground. He placed his ear a few inches from the earth. "People are coming. Four on horseback, one on foot."

"Now that you mention it," Hawkeye said, raising his ears, "I hear something, too. Uncas, I think your hearing is almost as sharp as my own. When it comes to smell, though, I've got you and your father beat for sure. When these folks get closer, we'll catch a good look at them."

Chingachgook and young Uncas pulled knives from the thin leather belts they wore around their waists. As Hawkeye waited by the stream, the Mohicans went about the task of skinning the deer. Hawkeye's little black nose, which was indeed very sensitive, sniffed in the fresh scent of the evergreen trees.

After about ten minutes, Hawkeye heard the men on horseback drawing near. The scout feared no beast in the forest. On the other hand, he knew men could turn out to be quite dangerous.

Hawkeye took a firm hold of his rifle. Chingachgook and Uncas also picked up their rifles. The three men moved through the trees. Soon they came to a narrow path that had been carved out by deer feet. The trees and brush were so thick that it was impossible to see more than a few yards down the path.

The galloping of horse hooves grew louder. Hawkeye held his rifle and cocked back the hammer— a metal device above the trigger. Then he called out in English, "Who comes?"

Moments later, an Indian not much older than Uncas appeared on the path, walking on foot. He wore a breechcloth and a necklace made of sharp bear claws. He wore his black hair the same way the two Mohicans did, indicating that he, too, was a warrior. There was something so frightening and cruel in the man's face that Hawkeye felt a shiver run through his fur.

Following behind the Indian came a man on horseback. He wore the uniform of an officer in the British army. It consisted of a scarlet-red jacket with gold trim; a three-cornered hat; and high black boots.

He was a very handsome young man, with the look of a gentleman.

Hawkeye set down his rifle. A British soldier was not a threat. Though Hawkeye did not approve of the war being fought, he sometimes lent a helping paw to the British side. The British forces, he figured, were like fleas in the fur, irritating but not deadly. The French forces, he thought, were a much more serious threat.

The officer spoke in a formal British accent. "I am Major Duncan Heyward, of the Sixtieth Regiment of the British army. Who are you, sir?"

"Oh, I'm just a common woodsman," Hawkeye answered. "You've nothing to fear from me or my friends. The fact is, we're somewhat friendly to members of the British army."

Major Heyward—or Duncan, as he was known informally—made a signal. Three more horses walked into view. Two of the horses were mounted sidesaddle by two finely dressed young women. On the third horse sat a very tall man who did not wear a uniform. The Indian in the group went to lean against a tree some distance away.

"These three travelers and I have come from Fort Edward," Duncan explained. "We are on our way to Fort William Henry. The two ladies are sisters and are going to visit their father, Colonel Munro. He is the commanding officer there. We left Fort Edward with several regiments of the British army who are also on their way to Fort William Henry. They are taking the wide path. However, for the safety of the ladies, I thought it would be wiser for us to travel another route. One never knows when there might be an ambush by the French. This Indian with us is serving as our guide. We left at dawn and should have been there by now. Do you know if we are near Fort William Henry yet?"

Hawkeye let loose a laugh. "Fort William Henry? Hoot, man! You are as much off the scent as a hound with a runny nose!"

"There is no need to make a joke of us," the major said with annoyance. "Even so, I fear you may be right. This Indian seems to have lost his way."

"That's mighty odd," Hawkeye said, glancing over at the Indian guide. "I've never heard of a red man losing his way in the woods. Who is this fellow?"

"His name is Magua," Duncan replied. "Like yourself, he is a friend to the British army. He is a Huron by birth, though he has been adopted by the Mohawk tribe."

Chingachgook and his son, Uncas, both held their rifles tighter. Hawkeye knew his friends did not trust members of either the Mohawk or Huron tribes. The Mohawks had fought in many bitter battles with the Mohicans in bygone days. The Hurons were even more fierce in their warlike ways. They had once been an honorable people. Now, however, the entire tribe seemed to have been infected with the poison of meanness.

Acting very casual, Hawkeye walked slowly over to the Indian called Magua. Hawkeye lowered his nose and gave the man a few sniffs around the ankles. The Indian just stared at the white man, showing no expression. When Hawkeye was done, he walked slowly back to Major Heyward.

"Here's the situation," Hawkeye told the major in a low voice. "You're not too far from Fort William Henry. I could take you there myself, but not right now. Not with night coming. And not with that Indian guide in our company. I suspect he's still more Huron than Mohawk. That means he's probably got the Huron meanness. I don't think this man is lost. I think he is trying to lead you and your fellow travelers into a deadly trap."

Duncan shot a suspicious look at the Indian guide. Sensing he was being discussed, the Indian darted away as fast as a spooked cat. He disappeared quickly through the tangle of brush and trees.

In the blink of an eye, Hawkeye seized his rifle and took aim. He wanted to slow Magua down by

shooting him in the leg. This would give the travelers more time to get away before Magua called upon the aid of his friends.

Unfortunately, Duncan and his horse moved into Hawkeye's line of fire. By the time Duncan cleared away, Magua was too far gone for Hawkeye to hit. The scout lowered his rifle without firing.

Duncan swung off his horse. His face was now as red as his uniform. "You're right. He was a villain. Let us give chase!"

Hawkeye slung his rifle across his furred back, where it hung by a leather strap. "It would be like chasing the wind. Right now, I'd say your time would be better spent traveling in the opposite direction from him."

Chingachgook and the youthful Uncas both frowned in the direction of the fleeing Huron. The other three travelers sat on their horses, all of them wearing frightened expressions.

Duncan pulled out a handkerchief and wiped his forehead. "Perhaps you are right. Well, at least we are now free of this man."

"Major, you are far from free of him," Hawkeye said with a chuckle. "Obviously, he had his heart set on doing you folks some harm. He won't give up so easy. I can guarantee it. Most like, he's got some friends nearby. He'll go round them up. Soon the whole pack will be on your trail. If they catch you, I suspect they'll be in the mood for some scalping."

One of the women covered her mouth with a gloved hand, as if she were about to weep. The other woman reached out to comfort her sister. The tall man bowed his head to pray. No doubt they were frightened by the mention of scalping. It was an Indian punishment in which a warrior cut a piece off the top of his victim's head with a tomahawk and kept it as a trophy.

As the rays of sunlight slipped away, darkness began to creep into the forest.

Duncan crouched by Hawkeye. "I am afraid, sir, we are in a helpless position. I don't know these woods. Neither do I understand the Indian ways. If you and your companions will guide us, I will pay whatever price you may demand."

"Naw, keep your money," Hawkeye said with a wave of his paw. "It's of no use to us out here. But we'll help you all the same. Our payment will be the adventure this trip is likely to bring us."

"The night is coming fast," Duncan said, trying to hide his nervousness. "Where shall we go?"

Hawkeye turned to his Indian friends and said something in the Mohican language. Chingachgook and Uncas both nodded.

"All right, listen," Hawkeye said, speaking loud enough so all four travelers could hear. "I'll act as your scout. My friends and I are going to get you out of this sticky situation—or we'll die trying. Keep as quiet as you can and follow me."

Hawkeye began to move his four paws along the earth of the darkening woods.

Chapter Three

A canoe glided silently down the Hudson River. The night had grown totally dark. The trees on either side of the river now appeared only as shaggy black silhouettes.

Hawkeye gripped a paddle, which he pulled through the water with smooth, even strokes. He steered the canoe from the rear. Major Duncan Heyward worked a paddle up front. In the middle of the canoe sat the two ladies and the very tall man.

A short while ago, Hawkeye had brought the travelers to the river. There he had pulled the canoe out of some bushes near the bank. The Mohicans had stayed behind to tie up the horses and finish preparing the deer for roasting.

"Fear not," Hawkeye assured his passengers. "There's no finer vessel than an Indian canoe. It's made of the best birch bark, sewn together with the toughest roots, and sealed watertight with the stickiest tree resin. A good thing, too, because the water's about to get a bit rough."

Before long, a distant roar was heard. The canoe

was traveling upstream. The water began rushing toward it with increasing force. Hawkeye felt water splashing up at his fur as he and Duncan paddled even harder. Here and there, the water formed into foaming, white whirlpools. Hawkeye had to work his paddle with great skill to keep the canoe from getting sucked into the circular swirls.

As the water turned more violent, the canoe neared a towering waterfall. Great sheets of water poured down with amazing power, pounding the river, flying wildly into the air. Hawkeye folded down his ears to muffle the waterfall's thunderous noise.

One of the ladies covered her eyes and cried, "Oh, dear, we'll be dashed to our death!"

"Hang on!" Hawkeye cried, as he lifted his paddle from the water. The canoe spun out of control, twirling around and around. Then it shot sideways and came to a sudden stop. The canoe rested in a calm patch of water right beside the waterfall.

The scout jumped out. He helped the others out of the canoe and onto a large, flattened rock that rose several feet out of the water.

After giving his fur a good shake, Hawkeye shouted, "Wait right here. I'll be back before you can say 'What the devil am I doing here?'"

With a laugh, Hawkeye leaped back into the canoe and paddled downriver by himself. About twenty minutes later, he returned with the Mohican father and son.

As the Mohicans tied the canoe to a boulder with a strong rope, Hawkeye turned to the puzzled travelers. "Now follow me, and watch your step."

Hawkeye walked across the rock. He was careful not to let his paw pads slide on the slippery surface. He approached another, massive rock. Then he found the opening of a narrow tunnel, which he entered. After taking a few steps, Hawkeye passed through a hanging blanket and came to the darkened section of a cavern.

"Most amazing," Duncan said, as he led the rest of the group into the area. "We are inside an island cave in the middle of the river."

"Yes, there are the waterfalls on two sides of us, and river above and below," Hawkeye said, after giving his fur another shake. "It's a secret hiding place only the Mohicans and I know about. You need to get a look at that waterfall in the daylight. It's something to see. It falls by no rule of nature at all. It leaps, tumbles, skips, and shoots. Here it's white as snow, there it's green as grass. At one spot it rumbles like an earthquake, and at another it ripples with as much delicacy as the lace on a lady's gown. Yes, sir, this waterfall's got a mind of its own. That's why I like it so much."

Fun fact: The waterfall Hawkeye describes really does exist today, though it is no longer so wild. It's called Glens Falls. There's now a city near it, with the same name. Most of this story takes place around the upper part of the Hudson River in what is now New York State. Back in the 1700s, most of North America was still untamed wilderness.

Soon Chingachgook and Uncas had a cozy fire burning. Over it, they roasted big chunks of the fresh deer meat. The four travelers sat on the ground, obviously glad to rest their tired bodies. Hawkeye lay down, his furred belly relaxed against the cool rock floor.

"Now that we're somewhat safe, and well on our way," Hawkeye told the travelers, "I think it's time for proper introductions. They call me Hawkeye. I was born and bred here in America. My two friends are from the Mohican tribe. The older man is Chingachgook, and the younger one is his son, Uncas. I've already met Major Duncan Heyward, but not the rest of you."

Hawkeye looked at the two women. Both of them were beautiful young ladies in their early twenties. Their long dresses were of a simple design, but they seemed to be expensively made.

Though sisters, the two women appeared to be quite different. One sister had dark brown hair pulled back with a ribbon, dark eyes, and a tanned face. The other sister had skin as pale and delicate-looking as porcelain, light blue eyes, and curling ringlets of golden hair. The blond sister seemed rather childlike. The dark-haired sister had a more mature look about her.

"My name is Cora Munro," the dark-haired sister said with an English accent. "And I think I speak for all of us when I thank you for your help."

Hawkeye gave a polite nod of his muzzle, then turned to the blond sister.

"My name is A-A-A . . ." the blond sister stammered.

Cora spoke for her. "My sister's name is Alice Munro. I don't think she has recovered from the shock of that canoe trip. But she is the baby of the family, so her reaction is allowed."

Everyone chuckled, including Alice. Duncan

reached over to squeeze Alice's hand. Hawkeye could see there was some romantic interest between the two of them.

Hawkeye turned to the very tall man. It seemed the man didn't quite know how to handle his long arms and legs. All of his movements were made in the clumsiest manner. The man wore a traditional waist-coat, tight pants, a wide-brimmed hat, and a pair of iron-rimmed spectacles.

"My name is David Gamut," the tall man said very formally. "I am a singer of psalms. I teach singing to the youths of a number of settlements. I am on my way south and figured I would travel in the company of these pleasant people."

"Singing, huh?" Hawkeye said with a tilt of his head. "'Tis a strange calling. But then every person has their gift, and I suppose that's yours."

"It is a fortunate thing that my parents named me David," the tall man remarked. "It's the same name as the shepherd David in the Bible, who first gave us the psalms."

Hawkeye gave his side a scratch with his paw. "Names are interesting things, aren't they? I think the Indians are better at it than we are. The Indian doesn't get his official name until he or she has shown what they're like. That way, they always get a name that fits. Why, the most cowardly white man I ever met went by the name of Lyon. And don't even get me started on his wife, who was named Patience."

Cora glanced at the Indians, who were cooking by the fire. "What are the meanings of 'Chingachgook' and 'Uncas'?"

"'Chingachgook' means 'Great Serpent,'" Hawk-eye explained. "That's because he understands the windings and turnings of human nature. 'Uncas' means 'Nimble Deer,' because of how gracefully the young fellow moves. Hey, Mr. Snake and Mr. Deer, how's that supper coming along? I'm starving!"

Chingachgook muttered a private joke about Hawkeye's appetite. His son, Uncas, laughed with glee at the remark.

"How did you get the name 'Hawkeye'?" Duncan asked, as he cleaned his boots with a handkerchief.

"The name was suggested by a man that I had to shoot," Hawkeye explained. "On account of the sharpness of my aim."

"What is the name you were born with?" David asked, as he shifted to get his long legs into a comfortable position.

"Nathaniel Bumpoo," Hawkeye said with some embarrassment. "But wait—it gets even funnier than that. Early on, folks took to calling me Natty Bumpoo."

Everyone had a good laugh at the name. After a little more chat, the Mohicans brought each person a thick slice of roasted meat. Hawkeye was so hungry that he tore into his meal and was easily the first one finished.

When dinner was done, everyone seemed happier and more relaxed. His tail wagging with satisfaction, Hawkeye said, "David Gamut, suppose you sing us one of your songs. It will be a friendly way of saying good-night."

David pulled a silver pitch pipe from his waistcoat and blew out a musical tone. He began to sing in a rich tenor voice. After a few notes, Duncan and the ladies lent their voices to the psalm, all four travelers singing:

> *How good it is, O see,*
> *And how it pleaseth well,*
> *Together, e'en in unity,*
> *For brethren so to dwell.*

Against the voices, the nearby waterfall rolled out its bass tone as if it were a church organ. Hawkeye sat there and brushed away a tear. The music reminded him of his youth, when he had lived with his parents in civilization. The scout opened his mouth to howl along with the psalm.

A frightening shriek pierced the night.

Everyone fell quiet. At first, Hawkeye thought the shriek had been his singing, which wasn't the finest. Then he realized it was something else.

"Wh-what was that?" Alice asked fearfully.

"I know the sound," Duncan whispered. "It's one of our horses screaming with terror. We left them not too far from here."

A wolf howled ferociously a few times. Then the howling faded gradually in the distance.

"Duncan, you were right," Hawkeye said, rising to his four feet. "That wolf was coming to attack the horses. But then the wolf ran away for some reason. That's fine for the horse, but probably not so good for us."

Cora put a protective arm around her younger sister. "Do you think that the wolf might have heard our enemies approaching?"

"Let's go find out," Hawkeye said. "Gentlemen, fetch your weapons and come with me."

The scout grabbed his rifle in his mouth and headed through the tunnel. Soon he stepped out onto the flat rock near the waterfall. The four other men of the group joined him there. Everyone crouched low so they would be difficult to spot. Duncan aimed his pistol forward, ready to shoot. David, who carried nothing but his pitch pipe, moved his lips in silent prayer. The Mohicans waited motionless with their rifles, as if they were made of stone.

Hawkeye took his rifle in his paws and cocked the hammer with his teeth. He put all his senses on full alert. In the dim moonlight, he saw nothing but the rushing river, and beyond the river, the dark shapes of the trees. He heard nothing but the continual roar of the waterfall. His nose smelled nothing but the sweet scents of nature. It seemed to be just another lovely summer night along the Hudson River.

The next instant, Hawkeye's tail shot straight up. The forest burst alive with frightening yells.

David sprang to his feet, shouting, "What in heaven's name is that?"

"Shh!" Hawkeye urged. "And get yourself—"

His warning was too late. From across the river came a steady round of gunshots, flashing fire and exploding with noise. David crumpled to the ground, clutching his side.

Hawkeye took aim with his rifle and squeezed the trigger. As the gun jolted, there was a shattering crack, and a leap of flame shot from the long barrel. The two Mohicans also fired their rifles. Duncan fired his pistol. Smoke floated through the air. Hawkeye's nose twitched at the bitter odor of burning gunpowder.

"Looks like Magua and his brothers found us," Hawkeye called out as the enemy gunfire continued. "Sounds like there's about three dozen of them. We don't need to kill them so much as just hold them back. Duncan, get David inside the cavern. I think the shot just grazed him."

Duncan crawled across the rock and pulled David into the cavern's safety. Hawkeye, Chingachgook, and Uncas moved to a cluster of jagged rocks that they could use for cover.

Hawkeye went about the slow process of reloading his rifle. Slung around his body, he kept a hollow ox horn filled with gunpowder and a pouch of bullets, which were really just lead balls.

The scout grabbed the horn, and he poured a bit of powder into the gun's barrel. Next, he grabbed a bullet and dropped it into his gun. He shook the rifle to spread the powder through the long barrel. He cocked the hammer. Fully prepared to shoot, Hawkeye bent back his ears and fired his rifle at the enemy. Then he began to reload.

Soon Duncan came out of the cavern and rejoined the battle. The shooting went back and forth for about fifteen minutes. Finally, Chingachgook, Uncas, and

Duncan all crept over to the scout. All of the men had run out of gunpowder.

"I've got some more stashed in the canoe," Hawkeye told the others. "Uncas, sneak your way over—"

The scout stopped. His whiskers twitched in a troubled way. Peering into the darkness, he saw the canoe floating downriver, guided by a Huron who swam alongside it. Hawkeye realized the canoe was being stolen. He and his men couldn't shoot the Huron at that distance, and there was no way they could go after him without getting shot themselves.

As the enemy gunfire came to an end, Hawkeye heard a savage shout of triumph come from the riverbank. He somehow got the feeling the shout had come from the mouth of Magua.

Uh-oh, Hawkeye thought. *This isn't too good.*

Hawkeye gave a signal with his paw, and his fellow fighters followed him through the tunnel. Back in the cavern, David leaned weakly against the wall.

"He'll be all right," Cora said, as she tied a strip of her dress around his wound.

"Duncan," Alice said with a trembling voice, "why do you look so worried?"

Duncan placed his pistol in his holster. "Our enemies have made off with our canoe, which contained the last of our gunpowder. I'm sorry to say that our situation has become rather desperate. We're trapped without the proper means to defend ourselves."

"Perhaps they've had enough fighting for the time," David managed to say.

Hawkeye shook his muzzle. "No. Once a wolf gets

a bite of meat, its appetite only grows. Believe me, I know. They will attack again. Perhaps in a minute, or perhaps in an hour. But sure as the sun, they will attack. They won't give in until they've taken every one of our scalps. I know I'm in need of a haircut, but I don't need one *that* badly."

Chingachgook and his son, Uncas, sat by the dying embers of the fire. Duncan wrapped a comforting arm around Alice's shoulders. A feeling of doom spread through the dark cavern. It was so thick the scout could smell it.

Cora knelt beside Hawkeye and placed a hand on his furred neck. "You and Chingachgook and Uncas can save yourselves. The rest of us could never get away. But I've no doubt the three of you could swim your way downriver."

"Perhaps," Hawkeye replied. "But we would rather die with honor than live with the shame of leaving you fine people behind. How could I deliver the news to your father?"

"My father, Colonel Munro!" Cora exclaimed, ruffling Hawkeye's fur. "That's it. You said yourself his fort is not too far from here. The three of you can slip away and get word to him. He'll send an entire regiment to rescue us!"

Hawkeye dug his paw at the rocky ground, considering this idea. It made some sense. He turned to the Mohicans and told them the idea in their own language.

"Good plan," Chingachgook said in English. Without another word, he picked up his rifle and passed through the blanket, leaving the cavern.

Hawkeye gestured with his paw. "Uncas, you go, too."

"I no go," the youthful Uncas said in English. "Uncas no leave ladies."

Cora went to Uncas and gave a gracious bow of her head. "You are a true gentleman, sir. But your skills will be put to better use by working for our rescue. I beg of you, please go. It is the best chance for us to meet again."

For a long moment, Cora and Uncas held each other with their eyes. Hawkeye got the feeling there might be a little romance brewing between them. Without another word, Uncas picked up his rifle and passed through the blanket.

Cora returned to David's side. Alice began to cry quietly against Duncan's shoulder.

Hawkeye pawed at the ground a moment, then spoke to the four travelers. "Now, listen to me. If you folks are killed before we return, I apologize now for our lateness. But there's a good chance you may be taken prisoner. If that happens, try to leave a sign of your trail. The best thing to do is to bend some branches on trees and bushes as you pass by. The ladies will have a better chance of doing this, as they won't be watched very carefully. All right, I suppose I've said enough. Best of luck to you folks. One way or another, I promise I will find you. For now, farewell."

Hawkeye gathered his rifle in his mouth and passed under the blanket. As he moved through the darkened tunnel, he felt his ears droop with sadness. The scout had come to think of the four strangers as friends. Though Hawkeye liked to remain hopeful, he knew there was a good chance he would never again see these four people alive.

Hawkeye and his Mohican friends will do their best to save the travelers from the scheming Magua.

Back in Oakdale, my friends and I are doing what we can to save Jackson Park. We've got a villain in our story, too, and we're just about to meet him.

Chapter Four

Wishbone led Joe, Sam, and David along a sidewalk in downtown Oakdale. They were headed for Leon King's office. There they hoped to uncover Mr. King's trick behind the purchase of the land in the park—if there was a trick.

"Let's pick up the pace," Wishbone called as he moved his paws faster. "We've got to settle this thing by noon. Oooh, I don't like or trust this King character one little bit. He's a—"

Wishbone leaped aside as he was almost trampled by a pair of shiny black shoes. He looked up to see the very person he had been talking about—Mr. Leon King.

"Oh . . . hi, there, Mr. King," Wishbone said somewhat cautiously. "I was just telling my friends . . . uh . . . let me see . . . What *was* I telling them?"

Mr. King stared down at Wishbone. The real estate developer was a middle-aged man who usually looked as neatly groomed as a dog-show champion. He wore an expensive double-breasted suit, a colorful tie, and every strand of his silvery hair was slicked into place perfectly. Wishbone's nose twitched as he picked up a heavy scent of cologne coming off the man.

Mr. King looked at the three kids, showing his overly white teeth with a smile. "Hello, there, kids. Beautiful morning, isn't it?"

Wishbone watched Mr. King carefully, in case he tried anything . . . sneaky. *He's smiling, but I know he doesn't like my friends—not after the way they stopped him from building his restaurant next to the park a few months ago.*

"Hello, Mr. King," Joe said, doing his best to sound friendly. "We heard you're planning to build a Tastee Oasis again. This time it's going to be inside the park."

Though Joe was being polite, Wishbone knew his buddy was after something—information that might reveal what kind of trick Mr. King had up his sleeve.

"Well, I'm not building the Tastee Oasis *in* the park," Mr. King said, as he smoothed his tie. "My lawyers examined the park's land deed, and then my surveyors checked the boundaries. You know what they discovered? Some of the land on the park's northeastern edge doesn't really belong to the park. It belongs to the same company that owns the property around Jack's Service Station. These guys didn't even know they owned this land. So I paid them a pretty penny and bought the property. Everything's been done perfectly legally."

"Are you sure it's perfectly legal?" Sam asked in a tone every bit as polite as Joe's.

Mr. King's eyes narrowed as he gazed at each of the three kids. Wishbone smelled a mixture of anger and nervousness creeping through King's cologne.

Suddenly Mr. King flashed his smile again. "Somehow I get the feeling you kids aren't so happy about my plan. Don't you want a Tastee Oasis? Just think about it. Beef burgers charbroiled to perfection. French fries cut from the freshest of potatoes. Ice-cream sundaes dripping through and through with the richest toppings."

Hey! He's not playing fair, Wishbone thought as he licked his chops. *My mouth is watering like a rainstorm.*

"Yes, we like that kind of food," David said, placing his hands in his pockets. "But aren't there plenty of other places where you can build the restaurant?"

"Sure, but that's the best location," Mr. King said, giving David a friendly pat on the back. "And location is everything in the real estate game. But here's what I'll do for you nice youngsters. When the restaurant opens, I'll treat each of you to a free meal. Can't beat that, can you?"

I smell something cooking—and it's not just hamburgers, Wishbone thought. *This guy may act smooth as ice cream, but I know he's as slippery as french fry grease. Yes, sir, he's got something up his sleeve, and he's trying to talk us out of finding it.*

"Uh . . . sorry," Joe said, sounding just a bit less friendly. "I don't think we will be coming to your Tastee Oasis—*if* the town council allows you to build it."

Mr. King's eyes turned cold as ice. "Well, plenty of other people will come. Fast food is one of the fastest

45

ways around to make fast money. And isn't that what makes this country so great? Money. Profit. Free enterprise. Okay, it was nice talking to you kids. And you know what? That dog ought to be on a leash!"

Mr. King walked away, his shiny black shoes clicking loudly on the sidewalk.

Wishbone growled in reply.

"Easy, boy," David said, kneeling to pet the dog. "We'll get the best of him."

Joe stared after Mr. King. "Did he give us a tipoff to his trick—the way Mr. Bloodgood said he might?"

"Hmmm . . ." Sam said thoughtfully. "He looked sort of nervous when I asked if he was sure his plan was perfectly legal. Which means it might *not* be legal."

"He also mentioned that this other company wasn't even aware it owned the land in the park," David pointed out. "That seems odd to me. Maybe we should examine the park's original land deed. Who knows? Maybe Mr. King found a way to twist its meaning somehow. There should be a copy of the deed on file at City Hall."

"I'm sure there is," Joe said, checking his watch. "But you have to go through a bunch of red tape to see it. And we don't have a lot of time. It's already ten-thirty. Maybe we can find the information we need at the library."

Wishbone leaped in front of his friends to lead the way to the library. "Great idea, Joe. Oh, I love books more than anything—with the possible exception of food. Hey, maybe we can grab a bite to eat on the way. No, sorry, forget it, we don't have time."

Speaking of running out of time, I sure hope Hawkeye and the Mohicans can help Cora, Alice, David, and Duncan before Magua discovers where they are hiding. Let's get on back to the banks of the Hudson River. I'm itching to find out what happens.

Chapter Five

The fire in the cavern had died out. As Major Duncan Heyward sat in the darkness, he kept reminding himself that he was not in the middle of a dream. It had been almost an hour since Hawkeye and the two Mohicans left the cavern. Since Duncan had heard no sounds of struggle, he figured the men had escaped successfully. This gave Duncan hope, as did the fact that so far no Hurons had discovered the secret hiding place.

Around the shadowy cavern, Duncan saw the frightened faces of dark-haired Cora, blond Alice, and the psalm-singer, David Gamut. Duncan knew these people were once again his responsibility.

Duncan's heart skipped a beat when he saw the blanket over the room's entrance being slowly lifted. Behind the blanket, the shape of a man appeared. The necklace of bear claws told Duncan the very worst—this was the dreaded Magua.

In a voice low and threatening, Magua said, "Come with me."

Having no choice, Duncan, Cora, Alice, and David followed Magua out of the cavern. Once outside in the night air, they were surrounded by about forty Huron warriors. Each wore on his face the designs of war applied by paint. Many of the Hurons let out fierce and bloodthirsty cries when they discovered that Hawkeye and the Mohicans were not in the cavern. There followed a brief discussion in the Huron language between Magua and the warrior who seemed to be the leader of the group.

"What are they discussing?" Alice whispered to Duncan.

"Probably whether to kill us or take us as prisoners," Duncan replied.

"Neither idea is a very cheery one," Cora commented.

"The Lord will see us through," David assured the others.

When the discussion ended, Magua led Duncan and his companions to where the stolen canoe had been docked. The captives boarded the canoe, along with Magua and another Huron. The two Hurons paddled the canoe downriver. The rest of the Hurons swam alongside it. Soon the canoe landed near the spot where the Mohicans had hidden the travelers' horses.

Cora and Alice were forced to get up on their horses. Duncan and David were forced to trade their boots for moccasins. Then Magua, Duncan, David, the Munro sisters, and five other Hurons set off through the darkened maze of the woods. The rest of the Hurons and the two remaining horses set off in another direction. It seemed that Duncan and his companions were to be prisoners left in Magua's evil hands.

After a few minutes of traveling, Duncan saw Cora reach out to bend the branch of a tree. Immediately, a Huron uttered a harsh warning, and Cora pulled her hand back. With a sinking heart, Duncan realized it would be almost impossible for Hawkeye to follow their trail. The Hurons had taken two separate paths, leaving Hawkeye to guess which path to follow. All footprints would be made only by moccasins, confusing Hawkeye into believing that all travelers were Indians. And there would be no telltale bending of tree branches.

The group hiked for hours, mostly in hushed silence. When the rosy blush of dawn colored the sky, Duncan decided to try something.

The major walked past the horses to bring himself alongside Magua. The Huron looked more threatening than he had during the night. His eyes were meaner, and now the upper half of his bronzed face was painted solid black, like the mask of an executioner.

"Tell me," Duncan said, knowing Magua spoke English fairly well, "what does the name 'Magua' mean?"

"It means 'fox,'" Magua said, pointing at his head. "For Magua has a very clever mind."

"You are clever, indeed," Duncan remarked. "It was most clever of you to capture these two women. They are very dear to their father, Colonel Munro. Their loss would tear his heart in half. I am sure he will pay you a great amount of gold for their safe return."

A smile flickered on Magua's lips. "I know loss of daughters will wound Colonel Munro. That is why I have taken them. I hate the man."

This was not welcome information to Duncan. He asked, "Why do you hate Colonel Munro?"

"I tell you Magua's story," Magua said as he walked, almost as if he were speaking of someone else. "Magua was born among the Huron tribe. He lived twenty summers before he ever saw a white man. He was brave and noble and marked to be great chief among his people.

"Then a group of French fur traders visit his camp. They give Magua something he had never seen before. You call it 'liquor.' We call it 'fire water.' It burns in the belly and mind. Magua drink too much of the fire water. He became a mean, lying rascal. He became so bad, his tribe drive him away like he was a raccoon. Magua walk far by himself. Then he find a new home with the Mohawks."

"So that's how you became a Mohawk," Duncan said, trying to act politely.

"When the war start," Magua continued, "Mohawks fight with British. So Magua fight along with British, too. He find himself in a camp under command of Colonel Munro. One night, Magua drink too much fire water and cause trouble in camp. Munro had him whipped like a dog."

"Drunkenness cannot be allowed in a military camp," Duncan pointed out to Magua. "Punishment was necessary."

Magua's voice thickened with anger. "I broke

51

rules only because I was slave to white man's fire water. When I drank fire water, I was no longer Magua. All the meanness you now see in red men comes from evil ways of the white man. Even scalping. Indians no scalp anyone before white man come. Indians only began to scalp because white man pay for scalps of enemies. Because white man want all of the land!"

"Yes, I'm afraid that is true," Duncan admitted with some embarrassment.

"Now I will take all your scalps," Magua snarled through gritted teeth. "And I will give them to Munro. That will be his punishment. And that will be my revenge!"

Alice gasped. Duncan turned to see that she and Cora had been listening from atop their horses.

Cora spoke calmly as she rode. "Magua, I understand your anger. If you must have revenge, take only my scalp and let the others go free. My death alone will be punishment enough for my father."

Magua took a few steps back so he could walk alongside of Cora's horse. Duncan did the same, to protect the women.

Magua looked up at Cora with a strange gleam in his eyes. "When Magua left his Huron tribe, his wife was given to another man. Now Magua has stopped drinking fire water and returned to his tribe. Now he only pretends to be Mohawk and friend of British. But now Magua needs new wife. He needs woman to take care of his wounds and hoe his fields of corn. If you will be my wife, I no kill any of you."

Alice covered her mouth with a hand. Duncan felt a desire to strike Magua, but he controlled himself.

"Magua, I would not love you," Cora said evenly. "Therefore, I would not be a good wife."

Magua placed a hand on the side of Cora's horse. "Magua beg you to be his wife. Because you are beautiful. And because that will rip the heart of Colonel Munro."

Cora pushed away Magua's hand. "Though you may have been a good man once, you are now a monster. I will never be your wife!"

Duncan saw anger cross Magua's face like a dark cloud. The Huron uttered a sharp cry. Instantly, the journey came to a stop, and Magua spoke to the other Hurons.

The group had arrived at a grassy meadow surrounded by trees. A bright sun had climbed above the horizon. Fleecy white clouds floated against a pure blue sky. Tree branches were alive with the cheerful chirping of a variety of birds. In that picturesque setting, the Hurons went about their task of stripping bark off nearby trees with their tomahawks. Duncan realized Magua was preparing to burn his prisoners alive.

Desperate to protect his friends, Duncan jumped at Magua. But, quick as lightning, Magua swung the blunt end of his tomahawk into Duncan's head. Instantly, Duncan fell unconscious.

When Duncan regained his senses, he found himself bound to a tree by a leather strap tied tightly around his shoulders. He saw that David, Cora, and Alice were bound to nearby trees in a similar way. At the feet of each prisoner lay a pile of dry tree bark. One of the Hurons was twirling one stick against another to create a spark of fire.

Magua walked up to Cora, clutching his tomahawk. With burning eyes, he said, "Your sister has bright yellow hair, like the corn. Will you be my wife and care for my fields of corn? Or do I send your sister's scalp to your father?"

Alice let out a pitiful wail.

"See, the child weeps," Magua told Cora. "She does not wish to die. Only you can save her."

Cora turned to her sister. "Alice, you have heard this man's offer. Tell me, what would you have me do?"

"Dear sister," Alice said with tears running down her cheeks, "we have lived together, and now we shall die together. You will not become his wife."

Cora turned a pair of steady eyes on Magua. "You have heard my sister. I will not be your wife."

"Then everyone die!" Magua cried savagely.

He hurled his tomahawk straight for Alice, who screamed with terror. The weapon struck in the tree just above Alice's head. A few blond ringlets of Alice's hair fell to the ground.

Duncan breathed with relief, seeing Alice was still alive. Then he saw another Huron raise his tomahawk, preparing to throw it at the same living target.

Gathering every ounce of his strength, Duncan broke free from his bonds. He flew at the Huron, sending both their bodies to the ground. The Huron threw Duncan onto his back and crushed his knee into Duncan's chest, pinning him down. Next the Huron pulled a gleaming knife from his belt. He raised the weapon high above Duncan's heart.

Major Duncan Heyward realized this was his last precious moment on earth.

A gunshot exploded.

The Huron fell face-down into the grass. With amazement, Duncan realized the Indian had been shot dead by a bullet.

Everyone stood frozen with shock.

"Who has saved me?" Duncan whispered under his breath.

Suddenly a figure burst through the trees across the meadow. The figure ran, keeping low to the ground, a rifle clamped in his mouth. Duncan realized his savior was Hawkeye!

The scout was followed by Chingachgook and his son, Uncas, each one gripping both a tomahawk and a knife.

Magua yanked out his knife. He moved his other hand back and forth against his mouth, all the while releasing a wild and frightening cry. Duncan recognized this as the Indian war whoop.

As the five Hurons ran to meet the attackers, Duncan rushed over to fetch the tomahawk that was still stuck above Alice's head.

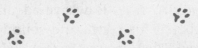

Hawkeye felt his paws pound against the grass as he charged toward the enemy. He saw the Hurons charging toward him with raised voices and ready weapons.

I won't have time to reload my rifle, Hawkeye thought, sizing up the situation as he ran. *Which is too bad. But they won't have time to fetch and load their rifles, either. Which is good. So this will be hand-to-hand combat. There's five of them against four of us. Which isn't too good, but not too bad, either. Here we go!*

The two sides met in the middle of the meadow. A furious whirlwind of battle began.

Magua slashed his knife at Chingachgook, who spun away. Then the Mohican plunged his knife at Magua.

Uncas grabbed a Huron around the neck and slammed him to the ground.

Duncan heaved his tomahawk at a Huron. The Indian ducked, then made a mad rush for Duncan.

As Hawkeye watched all these fights, a Huron ran straight toward him, carrying a wicked-looking club with a steel spike in it. Hawkeye swung his rifle at the man's legs and sent him flying to the ground. Next, Hawkeye clobbered the man on the back of the head, leaving him unconscious.

Before Hawkeye could catch his breath, a gigantic Huron was on the spot, snatching up the club. The man twirled it over his head, preparing to bring down a death blow on the scout.

Dropping his rifle, Hawkeye advanced toward the Huron, bared his teeth, and sounded his most ferocious growl. The Huron swung the club downward, but Hawkeye danced away just as the spike nailed into the ground. As the Huron lifted his club for another try, Hawkeye tripped the man. The Huron stumbled

backward and lost control of the spiked club, which turned and tore into his own chest. He lay on the ground, helpless to continue the fight.

Panting hard, Hawkeye looked around. He saw Uncas knock his opponent senseless. He also saw Duncan's opponent send Duncan tumbling over backward.

Then Duncan's opponent seized his tomahawk and hurried toward Cora. The Huron yanked Cora by her dark hair. Hawkeye ran over, but he knew he wouldn't make it in time. He saw the Huron pull back his tomahawk, all set to hack off Cora's scalp. Alice screamed, and David raised his voice in deep prayer.

Like an arrow, the young Uncas flew through the air and sent the Huron sprawling on his back. By the time Hawkeye reached the spot, Uncas had already cut the Huron's throat.

Next, Hawkeye, Uncas, and Duncan hurried over to help Chingachgook, who was wrestling on the ground with Magua. The two powerful men rolled back and forth in a cloud of dust. Hawkeye could see they were fighting for control of a knife. But their bodies were locked together in such a way that it was impossible to step in to help the Mohican.

Hawkeye's whiskers twitched nervously when he saw the blade touch Chingachgook's neck. But then Chingachgook tore the knife away and managed to jab it into Magua's side. Blood poured out of the wound, and the Huron released his grasp on the Mohican. Magua lay motionless, apparently dead.

"Well done," Duncan said, helping Chingachgook to his feet.

"Thank you," Chingachgook said in English.

"'Well done' is right," Hawkeye agreed, his tongue panting with exhaustion. "Magua's down, and so are the other four Hurons. Boys, we have won the battle!"

Hawkeye whipped his head around, seeing movement. Swift as a snake, Magua slithered away, then sprang to his feet. As if he had not been wounded, Magua was off and running through the trees.

"He was only faking!" Duncan cried with surprise. "Let us set out after him!"

Chingachgook and Uncas looked to Hawkeye.

"Naw, let him go," Hawkeye said, shaking his head. "He has no weapon or friends. He can't harm us now. But I'll tell you one thing—Magua is every bit as cunning as the fox he's named after."

Duncan hurried over to untie Alice, Cora, and David. Then all four of them fell to their knees in prayer. Chingachgook and Uncas looked up to the sky, offering a prayer of their own kind. As Hawkeye licked some blood from his paw, he murmured a prayer of thanks that every one of these people had survived.

Hawkeye glanced at the sun, which blazed overhead like an angel's halo. "All right, folks," he called out, "let's be on our way. We're farther from Fort William Henry than we were last night. And, for safety's sake, we need to take a roundabout route."

As Uncas helped the sisters onto their horses, Hawkeye and Chingachgook gathered up all of the Hurons' gunpowder. Then Hawkeye led the group across the meadow and into the protective shade of the woods.

"How did you find us?" Duncan asked the scout as the group moved along a narrow pathway.

"As soon as we left the cavern," Hawkeye explained, "we thought twice about going to the fort. By the time we brought some soldiers after you, it might have been too late. Instead, we lay in wait by the river. We heard you being captured. But there were so many hootin' Hurons that all we could do was hang back, then hope to pick up your trail later."

"That couldn't have been too easy," Duncan said. "They did much to throw you off the trail, and we did not have a chance to bend any branches."

Hawkeye swatted a mosquito. "No, it wasn't easy. When the path split into two directions, each with horse prints, I had no idea which way to go. Neither did Chingachgook. But Uncas, here—"

Uncas spoke up, trying to finish the story in English, a language that was difficult for him. "I study horse prints very careful. I know ladies ride on side of saddle. That make print to look just a little . . . oh, what is word?"

Cora smiled down from her horse. "I think the word you're looking for is *different*."

"Yes, different," Uncas said, returning Cora's smile. "So then I know which path to follow. Then we see man hunting. He give to us some gunpowder. We go fast and come just in time to, uh . . ."

Alice gave a giggle. "Save me from having all my pretty hair cut off with an axe."

Everyone laughed except for David Gamut, who trudged a ways behind the others. "I do not like this howling wilderness," David said, as he pushed his spectacles up on his nose. "It is far too dangerous, much too tiring, and I think I just received a mosquito bite!"

Hawkeye went back to give David a nudge with his muzzle. "Don't slow us down, David Gamut. We have a lot of ground to cover. Besides, your legs are at least twice as long as my own. And listen, Uncas, when you're done bragging to the ladies, perhaps you could keep a lookout for some food. After a rough-and-tumble fight, I'm usually hungry enough to swallow a bear!"

Chapter Six

With Hawkeye leading the way, the group journeyed onward. The scout frequently checked his route by examining the moss on the rocks, the direction of the streams, and the position of the sun. By following these clues, he could read the region like the back of his paw.

Gradually, the shady woods gave way to a landscape of rolling hills and valleys. Their rounded forms were carpeted with a wide variety of trees—pine, spruce, elm, beech, birch, aspen, and more. The hot, bright sun beamed down, showing the leaves to be every possible shade of green. Each time Hawkeye looked, he was able to pick out a color he had never noticed before.

"Oh, I just love trees," Hawkeye said, pausing to scratch his furred back against some bark. "They are useful for so many things."

Finally, the sun turned a fiery orange and began to sink behind a mountain range. The group stopped for supper and a few hours' sleep. Their resting spot was alongside a rundown building made of logs and sheets of bark.

Chingachgook and his son, Uncas, built a fire, then began roasting some deer meat. Hawkeye led Duncan, David, Cora, Alice, and the two horses to a stream whose water gurgled musically over a collection of rocks. Everyone drank until they had quenched their thirst. They also washed away some of the sweat and dirt from their many hours of travel.

"I wonder what that deserted building was used for," Major Duncan Heyward said as he wiped his boots clean.

"It's a little fort that I helped to build," Hawkeye replied, after lapping up some of the stream's fresh water. "When Chingachgook and I were much younger, we fought a battle on this ground. Between the Mohicans and the Mohawks. Many died on both sides, and their bodies are buried around here. I helped to dig the graves, too."

Night began to throw its veil of darkness across the forest. As the air cooled, the trees changed into big black shapes that resembled many-armed giants.

"Why were those two tribes fighting each other?" Cora asked, as she scrubbed her face with her sleeve.

Hawkeye sat on the ground, relaxing his four paws. "It's a sad story. The Indians have been living in this country for, oh, no one knows how long. Some say they traveled here from Asia way back, but no one knows for certain. But there was plenty of fertile land to go around.

"For the most part, all the different tribes got

along very well. You see, the Indians don't believe land can be owned. It's just there to be lived on and taken care of. And they're right. You don't see any borders or boundary lines drawn across nature."

"No, you don't," Cora said, sitting beside the scout.

"Then about a hundred and fifty years ago," Hawkeye went on, "the white men from Europe started coming to these parts. First came the Dutch, then the French and British. They got the Indians to trap the beavers and bears for them so they could sell the furs back in their homelands. But these Europeans sold so many furs that, after a while, there weren't enough beavers and bears to go around. Then the Mohawks and the Mohicans got to fighting over the few that were left. Soon they had an ugly little war going."

"That is a sad story," blond Alice remarked as she took a seat beside Duncan.

Hawkeye dug a paw at the ground as he continued. "Then more and more white men came. They built settlements and forts everywhere. Life got worse and worse for the Indians. The whites cheated Indians out of land, got them drunk with liquor, and passed on diseases to them that they had never even known existed before.

"Besides all that, the whites kept getting the Indian tribes to fight against each other. They got them to trade their bows and arrows for rifles so they could kill one another more violently, and quickly. All in the name of what is known as 'civilization.' I think that is my least favorite word."

"Civilization is not altogether a bad thing," said David Gamut, the psalm-singer, as he scratched several mosquito bites at the same time. "In my opinion, there is nothing more magnificent than a church or a schoolhouse."

"The forest is my church," Hawkeye said simply. "And the streams and trees are my books."

"You are also rather fond of your rifle," David said with disapproval.

Hawkeye put a slight growl into his voice. "Let me tell you something, friend. I never point my rifle at a fellow man unless there is no choice. I take up arms only when myself or someone I like is in serious danger. Even then, I don't much care for it. Civilization has made these woods a dangerous place. If you wish to survive here, you should probably trade that little tootin' pitch pipe of yours for a weapon."

David offered the scout his hand. "I am sorry, Hawkeye. After all, you have saved my life today."

"Oh, that's all right," Hawkeye said, shaking David's hand with his paw. "I suppose this wide country is big enough for both our opinions."

"Now is time for food and rest," Chingachgook called over in English. "When moon rise, we must walk again."

Everyone headed to the fire, where the Mohican father and son served another fine meal of deer meat. Again Hawkeye was the first one to finish. Then it was time for a few hours of sleep. Cora and Alice went inside the deserted fort. Young Uncas made them a comfortable bed of cut shrubbery. Then

Uncas, Duncan, and David lay down just outside the fort's wall.

Within minutes, all were asleep except for Hawkeye and Chingachgook. Hawkeye lay on the ground, cleaning his teeth by chewing on a pine branch that tasted faintly of vanilla. The darkness grew so deep that the surrounding trees were felt more than seen. The woods fell into a lullaby hush. It seemed all the birds and beasts and even the trees slept. Yet Hawkeye noticed the wide yellow eyes of an owl watching him from a high branch.

Chingachgook sat nearby with his legs crossed, his body still as a statue. However, Hawkeye knew his friend's senses were fully alert, allowing the peaceful spirit of the forest to enter and mix with his own spirit. Knowing Chingachgook would be an excellent watchdog, Hawkeye curled up and closed his eyes. He eased into sleep, soon dreaming of a highly exciting chase with a wildcat.

A little later, Hawkeye felt something touch his furred back. When he opened his eyes, Chingachgook whispered, "Someone comes."

Raising his ears, Hawkeye heard distant footsteps. Both men picked up their rifles and cocked them into readiness.

A half moon had climbed quietly into the night sky. By the moon's silvery glow, Hawkeye glimpsed a group of men moving through the trees. Hawkeye's tail flicked with concern when he recognized a Huron warrior from that morning's battle.

They're following our trail, Hawkeye thought, as he

forced his tail to be still. *They want revenge, and it's only a matter of seconds before they find us.*

Hawkeye bent back his ears and trained his rifle at the Hurons.

One of the Hurons knelt down beside a mound in the earth. Hawkeye knew this was where some of the Mohawks from the long-ago battle against the Mohicans were buried. The rest of the Hurons came over to examine the mound. A few of them spoke in low tones.

Next, a very surprising thing happened. The enemy Hurons turned around and began to walk in the same direction from which they had come. Soon they were swallowed by the night's darkness. Hawkeye's ears shifted with confusion.

Chingachgook pointed at the burial mound. "They know bodies of red men are buried there. They do not wish to fight on this ground out of respect for the dead. Even though red men fight other red men, there still blood bond that makes us brothers. White men not destroy bond completely."

"Lucky for us," Hawkeye said, as he set down his rifle.

Soon the others were awakened and the party continued its journey. Using his sharp senses and the moon's soft light, Hawkeye led the way. After several miles, the ground grew rugged with rocks. Placing his paws carefully, Hawkeye guided the group among the uneven surfaces, which had been carved into the earth millions of years ago. Before long, the group arrived at another mountain range, its jagged shape standing black against the starry sky.

"I'm fairly good at digging," Hawkeye said, as he picked a brier from his paw. "But not even I can dig through these mountains. Therefore, folks, it's time to climb."

Up and down, up and down, the group traveled, climbing over mountains that grew steeper by the minute. Hawkeye began to pant, and his paws felt heavy as stones. Even so, he knew the group would be safest if they could reach their destination before the morning hours. David and Duncan stumbled on, totally exhausted. The horses carrying the sisters were holding up quite well, though. As for the two Mohicans, they seemed as if they could climb forever.

When the first gray of dawn appeared, the travelers reached the peak of their final mountain. The edge of a vast lake lay below, its water smooth as the surface of a glass mirror. Puffs of vapor drifted up from the water's surface, lending the scene an almost magical appearance.

"Just look at that beautiful lake," Hawkeye said, his tired tail giving a few wags. "The French priests used to call it the Holy Lake, because they used it for their baptism ceremonies. I used to go swimming there on especially hot days. But then the British came along and named it Lake George, after their king. Now the lake is used mostly for transporting military supplies."

Along one shore of the lake stood a huge structure built of logs. Flying from a pole in front of the building was the "Union Jack" flag of Great Britain. This was Fort William Henry, the destination the group had almost lost their lives to reach.

"I see the fort!" Alice cried with excitement. "Cora, we're only a short distance away from Father!"

Hawkeye pointed. Between the travelers and the fort lay an entire city of large white tents. Atop one of the tents flew the "fleur de lis" flag of France. Near the tents stood a threatening row of cannons.

"We may be near the fort," Hawkeye remarked. "But before we get there, we've got to thread our way past several thousand French soldiers—not to mention the Indian allies they've got camped with them."

As if to underline the point, a cannon boomed, shattering the calm of the morning.

Whew! I'm a bit weary from all this traveling. But there's not a lot of time for rest when you've got two stories going on at once.

Let's hike back to Oakdale and see if we can find out anything about that land deed.

Chapter Seven

Wishbone moved quietly through an aisle of the library. On either side of him, shelves of books towered to the ceiling. Dogs weren't usually allowed in the public library, but Wishbone had special permission to go inside because Joe's mom was the reference librarian. Wishbone just wasn't allowed to chew the books or make too much noise—but then those rules also applied to humans.

As Joe, Sam, and David followed, Wishbone watched the many books go by. On the lowest shelf, he noticed a book titled *Southwestern Cooking. Oh, that looks like a good one. I should paw through it sometime.*

Wishbone rounded a corner, entering another aisle. The dog noticed a book titled *Caring for Your Cat. Nope, I don't think I'll be checking that out anytime soon.*

Wishbone's tail flicked nervously when he saw a familiar pair of shiny black shoes. He lifted his muzzle to see Leon King staring down at him. Just then, Joe, Sam, and David rounded the corner.

"Oh . . . uh . . . hi," Joe said, surprised to bump into Mr. King in an aisle of the library.

Mr. King smiled, but again Wishbone smelled a little fear seeping through the man's cologne. "So we meet again," Mr. King said, glancing at Wishbone. "And I see you still have your dog with you. I believe it's a violation of town law to have an animal in this building. Is it not?"

"He's a friend of the librarian," Joe said, with a bit of irritation. "And the librarian happens to be my mom."

"It's nice to have friends in high places," Mr. King said with a chuckle.

"We didn't expect to see you here," Sam told him.

"Why is that?' Mr. King said, as he smoothed his tie. "Don't you think a guy like me likes to read?"

Wishbone said, "Frankly, King, I don't think you like to read anything but your bank statement."

"What are you looking for?" David asked innocently. "Maybe we could help."

"Oh, that's all right," Mr. King replied. "I'm done already." He showed a wide smile. Then he quickly walked away, his shoes clicking loudly on the tile floor.

"What was he *really* doing here?" Joe whispered to his friends. "I wonder if it could have something to do with his land deal. Maybe it's something he doesn't want us to know about. He did seem kind of uncomfortable when he saw us."

Sam scanned a shelf and pulled an old leather-bound book from it. Wishbone saw that it was titled *Oakdale—A Little Town with a Big History*. "Hey!" she said. "I think this might have some information about that land deed for the park."

The kids took the book to a nearby reading table and sat down. Wishbone jumped into a chair next to Sam to watch the action. As Sam checked the book's index, Wishbone leaned his muzzle in to get a better view. A lady at the next table stared at Wishbone with a curious expression, as if she were surprised to see a dog studying a book.

What does she think a library is for? Wishbone thought.

Sam leafed through the book and stopped at a certain page. "Here's something," she said eagerly. "I'll read it out loud. 'In 1874, Josiah Jackson donated one hundred and seventy-eight acres just west of downtown Oakdale to be used as a public park. The boundaries on each side were surveyed off the original post office building. After the deed was made final, Jackson stated, "No matter how large this town grows, it

should always have an area where the people can enjoy the sweet sights and smells of nature."' And . . . that's all it says on the subject of the deed."

Wishbone knew about the old post office, which stood at the very edge of the downtown area. It was a small wooden structure that had been built more than a century ago. When the town built a larger, more modern post office, the old one was kept for the sake of local history.

Joe wrinkled his brow. "What does it mean when it says, 'The boundaries on each side were surveyed off the original post office building.'"

Wishbone looked to David, knowing he would have the answer. "Well," David explained, "land deeds usually use some fixed point as a landmark, like a building or a tree. Then calculations are made off of that fixed point to figure out the boundaries in the deed. In this case, the fixed point is the old post office. Those guys we saw in the park were surveyors, and that device they were using is called a surveyor's level."

Joe tapped his fingers on the table. "So they would be measuring off the fixed point of the old post office, right?"

"That's right," David said with a nod.

"Well," Sam said, closing the book, "I don't see how this helps us figure out Mr. King's trick—unless he somehow moved the old post office. But I don't think that's too likely."

Joe continued tapping his fingers. "I wonder what Mr. King was doing here in the library."

"It's eleven-oh-five," David said, checking his

watch. "Remember, we need to figure this out by noon."

Wishbone's tail swished back and forth with concern. "Come on, everybody, we need to think of something. We can't let Mr. King ruin the park. Think, think, think!"

"How about this?" Joe suggested. "You two stay here and keep searching for something useful. Meanwhile, Wishbone and I will try to pick up Mr. King's trail and find why he was really in the library. And remember, we're meeting Mr. Bloodgood in front of city hall at a quarter to twelve. If we haven't found anything by then, at least we can speak our mind to the mayor and the town council."

"That's what I love about this country," Wishbone said as he jumped off his chair. "In America, every person and dog is free to voice an opinion. Let's get moving, Joe."

Wishbone and Joe walked quickly but quietly out of the library.

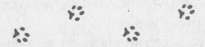

While we leave the quiet of the library, Hawkeye and his friends are about to enter a very noisy fort.

Chapter Eight

Cannons blasted away from the direction of the French camp, and cannons blasted back from the British fort. The explosions lit up the dawn sky as if part of a festive fireworks display.

Hawkeye stood with Chingachgook, Uncas, Duncan, David, Cora, and Alice at the bottom of a mountain, right near the battlefield. "Let's go!" Hawkeye yelled. "The French soldiers are so busy fighting, perhaps we can sneak right past them to the fort. It's no fun crossing a war zone, but we've no choice. Follow me. Stay as low as you can!"

Hawkeye began to crawl on his belly. He pulled himself along on all four paws. The others followed in the same way, pulling themselves along with their arms and legs. The ground rumbled from the never-ending cannon fire. Each explosion was as loud as a boom of thunder. Hawkeye's sensitive ears shook with every shot. A cannonball landed and exploded several feet in front of Hawkeye's muzzle, filling his black nose with spraying dirt.

"Don't slow down!" Hawkeye called back to his friends. "Last one to the fort has to cook supper!"

The plan worked. Soon Hawkeye and the others reached the high wooden fence that surrounded Fort William Henry. The scout scratched desperately at the fort's gate. "Open up! Let us inside!" he cried over the deafening noise of the battle.

"Father, it's us!" Cora shouted. "It your daughters— Cora and Alice! Please, open the gates!"

The gate swung open. Hawkeye and the others rushed inside, eager as dogs escaping a rainstorm. A British soldier led the group through a courtyard, then through a second wooden gate. The group was now inside the fort building, everyone still in one piece.

Hawkeye felt his whiskers twitch. The place smelled of sweat, blood, gunpowder, and human terror. Screaming was a common sound. British soldiers were running around frantically, their faces blackened with smoke. Ladders led up to a second story, where many of the soldiers were firing rifles and cannons at the enemy. Other soldiers were busy hauling supplies and tending to the wounded. Hawkeye noticed a few Indians and American colonists assisting with the fight.

A gray-haired man wearing the uniform of a British officer rushed over. He was big fellow who looked as if he could crush rocks with his bare hands.

"Father!" Cora and Alice cried out together.

Colonel Munro took both daughters into his arms and held them as if he would never let go. "Oh, my dear daughters!" he said with great emotion.

"I thank the Lord you have been able to get to me. Perhaps your mother in heaven was watching over you!"

David Gamut blew his pitch pipe and began singing a psalm of thankfulness.

Hawkeye's tail began wagging. The scout was very happy that he had helped to bring the sisters into the arms of their father. He didn't think this was a good place for the ladies to be, but he knew that wives, children, servants, and other regular citizens often stayed with soldiers in military forts.

Major Duncan Heyward introduced Hawkeye and the two Mohicans to Colonel Munro. Then Duncan asked anxiously, "Have the reinforcements come from Fort Edward?"

Colonel Munro shook his head. "No, confound it. General Webb and his men seem to have forgotten us. And we are terribly in need of them. Right now the combined forces of the French and Indians outnumber us five to one. If the men don't get here soon, we shall lose this fort. And we very much need a fort located on the lake's southern shore!"

"General Webb and his men left Fort Edward at the same time we did," Duncan said with a worried look. "They should have been here by now. I'd say they either ran into trouble, or . . . they have changed their mind about coming to your assistance."

A cannonball struck the fort, causing several planks of wood to come tumbling down.

"Can't say I blame them," Hawkeye remarked, as he pulled a paw out of the way.

"I do not like war," Chingachgook muttered to Uncas in Mohican.

"Me, either," Uncas told his father.

Colonel Munro's face took on the hard expression of a man who had seen too much of war himself. "The situation is most serious. I need to send someone to find out what has happened to General Webb. But it can't be just any man. I need a man who knows every inch of this area. A man who knows how to defend himself. And a man who is foolish enough to accept the assignment."

Hawkeye thought a moment, then raised a paw. "Uh . . . well . . . I suppose that would be me."

Several days later, Hawkeye was sorry he had volunteered for the mission. He found himself a prisoner in one of the French army's tents. He had been tied to a stake by a leashlike device.

The scout had managed to find General Webb. The man had taken his troops back to Fort Edward, the place from which Duncan and his companions had traveled. There the general gave Hawkeye a letter to deliver to Colonel Munro. The letter stated that Webb had changed his mind about sending men to help Munro. However, this night, on the way back to Fort William Henry, the scout had been captured by a group of French soldiers.

This wouldn't have happened if I had kept Chingachgook and Uncas by my side, Hawkeye thought with frustration. *But I didn't want them to get too mixed up in this white man's war nonsense. Hoot! I hate wearing a leash more than anything!*

Several men stood guard in the large tent. Though soldiers, they wore elegant, stylish white coats with pink trim. Seated at a desk was a middle-aged man dressed even more elegantly. He wore a light blue coat with yellow trim, and he had a large jeweled cross around his neck. To Hawkeye, the men looked more like they were dressed for a ball than a war.

The man at the desk was Louis Joseph de Montcalm. Not only was he a marquis, a royal position similar to that of a duke, but he was the commander of the French forces in the area. In one hand he held a glass of red wine; in the other, he held a letter, which Montcalm read with great interest. It was the letter Hawkeye had received from General Webb.

That letter ought to make him happy, Hawkeye thought. *It'll tell him that the men at Fort Henry won't be getting any assistance from Fort Edward. . . .* Hawkeye was distracted by the smell of food. *Boy, I'm starving!*

"Hey, Marquis!" Hawkeye called out. "Do you have anything to eat around here? Some roasted pheasant with wine sauce? Some crêpes Suzette? A bone with a little meat on it?"

Before Montcalm could answer, several French soldiers entered the tent. They were followed by a British officer. Hawkeye immediately recognized the man as Major Duncan Heyward. Duncan looked at Hawkeye, who shrugged his front paws as if to say "Sorry about getting captured."

Duncan bowed to Montcalm. The marquis rose from his seat and gave an even deeper bow in return.

"Marquis of Montcalm," Duncan announced, "I am Major Duncan Heyward of the British army. I suspected you had captured this messenger. I am here to seek his immediate release."

Montcalm returned to his chair, inviting Duncan to take a seat near the desk. He spoke in English, but with a thick French accent. "I am quite delighted that you have come, Major, because I have a request to make of *you*. I wish for the British army to surrender Fort William Henry to the French forces."

Duncan's eyes hardened. "We will not surrender."

Hawkeye watched closely.

Montcalm took a sip of wine, then continued. "I beg of you, listen to reason. The British have only two thousand men in their camp. I have eight thousand French soldiers and almost two thousand Indian allies from a number of tribes. I know you are expecting General Webb to send you several thousand men, but that will not be happening. As you will see."

Montcalm handed the letter to Duncan. After Duncan studied the letter, he looked to Hawkeye, who nodded his muzzle to indicate the letter was not a fake.

"Despite this letter," Duncan said, attempting not to show his feeling of hopelessness, "honor forbids the British from surrendering the fort."

"My dear major," Montcalm said with a courteous smile, "I do not wish to rob you of your honor—only your fort. I am prepared to offer the most generous of terms. If the British surrender, every man, woman, and child in the British camp shall be free to leave this place in perfect peace."

Hawkeye lifted his nose into the air, catching an unwelcome smell. He turned to see a man hovering in the darkness just outside of the tent, eavesdropping on the conversation. The scout's fur bristled when he saw the man's necklace of bear claws. He realized the man was Magua. Hawkeye knew the Hurons were among the Indian tribes that fought with the French.

Duncan set the letter on the desk and stood. "Marquis of Montcalm, your offer is most generous, indeed. You will have an answer from Colonel Munro tonight."

"Thank you," Montcalm said with a bow of his head. "And please take this messenger with you."

After Hawkeye was released, he and Duncan walked out of the tent. As the scout paused to scratch his neck where the leash had been, he asked, "Do you think Colonel Munro will accept all of the terms of surrender?"

"I am quite certain he will," Duncan said with sadness. "There's no way to stop the French from taking the fort, and Montcalm has offered the most favorable terms."

"Perhaps too favorable," Hawkeye said, as the two men moved among the many tents of the French camp. "I don't trust these French fellows, with their fancy clothes and fancy manners. There's another problem, too. I saw Magua around here a few minutes ago. I'm concerned he might stir up some trouble with all the Indians here in the camp. We both know how much he hates Colonel Munro. If and when the surrender happens, I urge you to keep a very careful watch on everything."

"Yes, I will," Duncan replied. "Will you be returning with me to the fort?"

"No, I don't think so," Hawkeye said, coming to a stop. "I've had enough of this awful war business. I'm itching to get back into the woods and find Chingachgook and Uncas. I'd be grateful if you would say good-bye to David and the sisters for me. And, Major, it has been a pleasure to know you."

Duncan gave Hawkeye a military salute. Hawkeye returned the salute with his front paw.

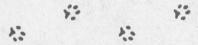

As a brilliant morning sun rose over Lake George, Duncan heard the stirring rattle of military drums. The night before, Colonel Munro had agreed to surrender Fort William Henry, and the surrendering ceremony was under way.

A bird flying overhead would have been treated to quite a colorful sight. Duncan and Colonel Munro led the procession marching out of the fort. Following behind them were two thousand scarlet-coated British soldiers. Behind them were the Indian and American colonial fighters and the several hundred members of the fort's civilian population. Every person was on foot, except for the sick and wounded, who rode on horseback. They were moving across a grassy plain that seemed to be made of green velvet.

On either side of the parade stood a sea of white-coated French soldiers and their blue-coated officers. Their number totaled almost eight thousand. Montcalm stood in front, wearing a hat with a decorative white feather.

Following Hawkeye's warning, Duncan kept a close watch in all directions. His eyes searched for any sign of trouble. Duncan would rather have been marching alongside Cora and Alice, but his military responsibility required that he march at the head of the procession. He had instructed David Gamut, the psalm-singer, to stay near the sisters at all times.

So far, all went well. Montcalm and his troops seemed to be treating the defeated army with the greatest of respect.

Duncan turned to Colonel Munro. The man carried himself nobly, but Duncan knew he was deeply shamed by the surrender. "Sir, there is one bit of happy news," Duncan said, hoping to cheer up the colonel. "I should like to marry your daughter."

"Ah, that is happy news," Colonel Munro said, managing a faint smile. "Cora could not make a better match."

"Actually, sir," Duncan pointed out politely, "the daughter I would like to marry is Alice."

Munro raised his eyebrows. "I see. Yes, I suppose Cora is a bit too independent-minded for most men. Very well. I suppose I've lost the fort, but gained a son."

The British procession was headed for the nearby woods. There they would follow the pathway to Fort

Edward. Duncan noticed the Indian allies of the French watching the ceremony from the shaded shelter of the woods. Suddenly, Duncan's blood ran cold. He had caught sight of Magua. The Huron was glaring at Colonel Munro in such a way that Duncan knew the man was up to something bad. Duncan placed a ready hand on his pistol.

Magua raised a hand to his mouth and released the frightening Indian war whoop. Others joined in, until several hundred voices were tearing the air with their whoops. It was the most horrifying noise Duncan had ever heard.

At once, a great mass of Indians rushed out of the woods, showing rifles, tomahawks, knives, spiked clubs, and spiteful eyes.

"What is happening?" Colonel Munro cried with alarm.

"I fear they are attacking us!" Duncan called back.

"I must speak to Montcalm at once," Munro said, stepping out of line. "He assured me no harm would come to anyone!"

By now the Indians were savagely attacking the British soldiers with their weapons. The British fought back as best they could, but most of them were completely out of ammunition. Duncan saw Munro running toward Montcalm, and he saw a few French soldiers attempting to assist the British. But the Indian attack was so vicious that Duncan doubted Montcalm would be able to stop it—even if he wanted to.

Duncan saw an Indian bash a nearby soldier in the face with a tomahawk. As blood flowed down the man's forehead, Duncan shot the Indian dead with his pistol. Then Duncan noticed a great number of Indians running toward the back of the line, where the women and children were.

Frantically, Duncan dashed in that direction, shouting, "Cora! Alice! Where are you? Cora! My beloved Alice!"

The cry was lost among the whoops, shouts, gunshots, groans, and screams that overpowered the scene. The peaceful surrender had turned into a bloody massacre.

I'm sorry to report that the massacre at Fort William Henry really happened. And, by the way, Colonel Munro and the Marquis of Montcalm really were the commanding officers at the scene.

No one is sure why the massacre took place. Perhaps Montcalm secretly ordered the Indians to attack, or perhaps they just did so on their own. It's not known exactly how many people were killed that fateful morning, but it could have been well over a thousand souls.

As the sun lowered over Lake George three days later, the plain lay still and quiet. Many, many dead bodies were scattered across the ground, their blood having stained much of the green grass. Behind the bodies stood the burned and smoking ruins of Fort William Henry.

Hawkeye, Chingachgook, and his son, Uncas,

moved slowly over the plain. The scout was sickened by the sights before him.

"Never have I seen such a crime as this," Hawkeye whispered to his Mohican friends.

The Mohicans said nothing, but their eyes were filled with quiet disgust.

Through the gloomy twilight, Hawkeye noticed two men kneeling on the ground. He and Chingachgook trotted over to them. Hawkeye saw that the two men were Major Duncan Heyward and Colonel Munro. Both had traded their military uniforms for woodsmen's clothing. The two men looked numb from grief and shock.

Hawkeye said, "We heard about the massacre and came to see for ourselves."

Duncan spoke in a weary voice. "Those fortunate enough to escape death made their way to Fort Edward.

The colonel and I returned here a few hours ago to search for our loved ones. We exchanged our uniforms for this clothing in the event some of the villainous Indians stumbled upon us."

"Are Cora, Alice, and David safe?" Hawkeye asked.

"They didn't make it to the fort," Duncan replied, "but we have not yet found their bodies among the dead," Duncan replied. "I hold some hope that they are alive."

Munro no longer looked like a heroic British colonel. He looked like a shattered man. In a trembling voice, he said, "My daughters, my precious daughters. Where are they?"

Uncas, who was now in the nearby woods, gave a shout. Hawkeye, Chingachgook, Duncan, and Munro ran over to see what the Indian had found. Uncas pointed to a green ribbon that rested on a bush. Hawkeye recognized it as the ribbon Cora had worn in her dark hair.

"I think Magua take Cora and Alice," Uncas said in English. "Could be David, too."

"Alas," Munro said, as he took the ribbon in his hand. "Then he has probably killed them by now."

"I think not," Chingachgook offered. "If Magua want to kill them, he kill them here. But he not done this. They are alive. For now."

Hawkeye put his nose to the ground, and he sniffed here and there. He picked up feminine scents that he now recognized as belonging to the Munro sisters. He pointed with his muzzle and said, "They went thataway. Trust me. I have a nose for this sort of thing."

Colonel Munro clutched Cora's ribbon desperately to his big chest. "Give me my children. I will pay any price to have my children back in my arms!"

Duncan knelt down to Hawkeye. "Where do you think they have gone?"

Hawkeye dug at the ground with his paw, thinking. "My guess is that they've gone north toward the Huron villages of the Canada territory. But it won't be easy to find them. Magua has probably zigzagged all over the place to throw us off the trail. But this matters not. I consider those three people friends of mine, and I've always been faithful to my friends. I will find those folks if I have to follow them to the ends of the earth. That is a promise."

The plot grows darker and deeper and, well, a bit scarier. But we need to stay on the trail, no matter where it may lead.

Joe and I also need to stay on the trail of sneaky Mr. King. So come on along and see what's going to happen next.

Chapter Nine

The second Wishbone stepped out of the library, he put his trusty nose to the ground and followed the scent of Mr. King's cologne. After a few blocks, the trail led to an office building in Oakdale's business district.

"Great job, boy!" Joe said, giving Wishbone a grateful scratch. "This must be where Mr. King's company is located. He probably is in his office. I wonder if we should go . . . No—here he comes! Let's hide!"

As Wishbone and Joe ran to hide behind a parked car, Mr. King stepped out of the building.

"I'm going to follow him," Joe whispered to himself.

Staying a good distance behind, Wishbone and Joe followed Mr. King down the block to the First Commerce Bank of Oakdale. When Mr. King went inside, Wishbone and Joe kept an eye on him from the bank's window.

After waiting in line, Mr. King went to one of the teller windows. He signed a form. Then the teller handed him a stack of paper bills. Mr. King pulled an envelope out of his suit jacket and placed the bills inside.

"That's interesting," Joe said to himself. "Why did he put the money in an envelope instead of in his wallet?"

"That's terribly interesting," Wishbone told Joe. "Wait a second. *Why* is that so interesting?"

Joe put a hand to his head, as if making a big discovery. "Maybe he put the money in an envelope because he doesn't plan to keep it. Could it be *bribe money* that he's planning to give to the surveyors working in the park?"

"Yes! That *must* be it!" Wishbone said, his tongue panting with excitement. "He's planning to pay them off so they'll say exactly what he wants to them to say about the land measurements. Good thinking, Joe!"

As Mr. King stepped out of the bank, Wishbone and Joe ran for cover at the side of the bank building. Peering out, Wishbone watched Mr. King walk next door to the Oakdale Attic Antiques store. When Mr. King went inside, Wishbone and Joe moved to watch through the store's window. Mr. King went over to an elderly woman who stood behind the counter.

Wishbone lifted his ears to hear the conversation. His hearing was sensitive enough to penetrate through most walls.

"I've decided to buy those diamond earrings, after all," Mr. King told the lady. "I think they'll make a very nice anniversary present for my wife."

"They certainly will," the lady said, taking a pair of earrings from the glass case on top of the counter. "How would you like to pay for this?"

Mr. King set the envelope of bills on the counter. "I'll pay with cash. My wife balances our checkbook and pays the credit-card bills. I'd rather she not see what I paid for the gift."

The lady took the bills, then gave Mr. King some change.

Wishbone's ears drooped with disappointment.

"Darn!" Joe said, punching the air with his fist. "It looks like he's not planning a bribe, after all. He's just using the money to buy jewelry. Well, come on, Wishbone, it's eleven forty-five. We'd better get over to city hall."

Wishbone and Joe walked the short distance to the red-brick city hall building. Just as they got there, Sam and David came running over.

"Did you find out anything?" Sam asked as she caught her breath.

"No," Joe muttered.

"But King's wife ought to be happy," Wishbone

added. "She's getting a pair of diamond earrings as an anniversary present. Myself, I'd prefer something chewable."

"Well, we found out something interesting," David said eagerly. "We looked—"

David stopped as Mr. King came walking along the sidewalk. Mr. King gave the kids a little salute, then disappeared inside city hall.

"We looked through a few more books," David continued, "but we didn't find anything useful. But then we took another look at that first book, *Oakdale— A Little Town with a Big History.* We discovered that one of the pages had been torn out. We found two more copies of the book, but each one had *the same page* torn out."

"We think Mr. King might have been the one who tore out those pages," Sam added. "That might have been what he was doing at the library. Maybe he knew those pages revealed something he didn't want anyone else to know. When he saw we were checking into this land deal, he got nervous and went straight to the library to remove the evidence. Unfortunately, we have no way to find out what was on that page. Your mom said the library had only three copies of the book."

Mr. Bloodgood came hurrying over, his long black hair waving in the breeze. "Okay, folks, it's almost noon. How did you kids make out?"

"I think we got real close to something," Joe said sadly. "But not close enough. And we're out of time."

"That's all right," Mr. Bloodgood said, giving Joe's arm a squeeze. "You guys did your best. Besides, maybe we can win the mayor and town council over to our side. On the way in, you can tell me what you discovered."

Joe knelt down to give Wishbone a few pats. "You'd better wait right here, boy. The last time I brought you into city hall, we got a lot of funny looks. I don't think dogs are too welcome there."

Wishbone watched the group head for the city hall building. *No dogs, huh? Well, that's the first rule I'll change when I finally get myself elected mayor of this town. But right now I might be more valuable working on the outside. I know a way that might allow me to get my paws on one of those missing pages. After Mr. King left the library, he went to his office. I'm thinking maybe he hid the pages in there somewhere. Let's see . . . What was the address of that building? Oh, why don't I just follow Mr. King's smell?*

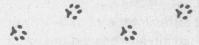

While I backtrack on the trail of Mr. King, Hawkeye and his friends follow the trail of Magua and the sisters.

Have you noticed there's a lot of trail-following going on? Fortunately, we all have good noses.

Chapter Ten

As stars glittered in the night sky, the birch-bark canoe glided through the still waters of Lake George. Hawkeye and his team of Chingachgook, Uncas, and Duncan were off in search of Magua and his prisoners.

Colonel Munro was too grief-stricken to make the journey. He had already headed to Fort Edward, where he would wait for news of his daughters. As dawn arrived, Hawkeye and his men docked the canoe on the lake's northeastern shore.

They were near the border of the Canada territory, in a region of forest where very few white men had ever set foot.

"All right, boys," Hawkeye said in English, as he shook some water from his fur. "We need to pick up Magua's trail. It'll be tough but, I tell you, not even a hummingbird flies without leaving some sign of its path. Let's get to work."

As the group hiked through the dense woods, Hawkeye and the Mohicans studied the passing trees, bushes, dirt, sticks, fallen leaves, and even rocks. By the time the sun had traveled all the way across the sky, the men had found no sign of the people they were after. They kept at their task, though, like dogs in search of buried bones.

By nightfall, Chingachgook discovered many sets of footprints, and two sets of horse hoof prints. Uncas, his son, recognized the hoof prints as belonging to the same two horses the sisters had ridden to Fort William Henry.

"It's the right trail," Hawkeye said, lowering his black nose to the ground. "I can also smell the gentle scent of the ladies. Well done, boys. How about celebrating with a bite to eat!"

After supper and a few hours' sleep, Hawkeye and his men were up with the sun, once more following the trail. As Hawkeye had expected, the pathway twisted and turned so much that he frequently felt as if he were chasing his own tail.

As sunset fell, the trail seemed to disappear. Hawkeye felt his tail droop with disappointment, but Uncas was not discouraged. Kneeling by a shallow stream, the young Mohican built a small dam from sand that changed the water's course. As the streambed turned dry, footprints revealed themselves.

"Ah, that was a clever trick, Magua!" Hawkeye exclaimed, his tail wagging with excitement. "But not clever enough to fool the likes of us. Onward, boys!"

Hawkeye and his men followed the footprints to a pond surrounded by odd miniature mud huts.

"It's a beaver village," Major Duncan Heyward

announced as he watched several beavers scurrying out of the water to enter their cozy homes.

Through the twilight, Hawkeye caught sight of a very tall Indian a distance beyond the pond. Chuckling to himself, he crept quietly toward the Indian, who was so busy watching the beavers he didn't notice the scout's approach. Hawkeye grabbed a piece of the Indian's legging in his teeth.

"Ahhh!" the Indian shouted as he tried to pull free from the grasping teeth.

As Hawkeye knew, the Indian was not really an Indian. It was David Gamut, the psalm-singer, with the clothing and shaved head of an Indian warrior. The biggest giveaway was the Indian's very civilized iron-rimmed spectacles.

"How now, friend," Hawkeye said with a big grin.

David smiled upon recognizing the scout. "How now yourself. It's excellent to see you!"

Hawkeye put a paw to his mouth and made a snakelike hissing sound. This was a signal for the others to approach, which they did. Chingachgook and Uncas snickered at David's Indian appearance. After realizing the Indian was really David, Duncan asked eagerly, "What has become of the sisters?"

"In the middle of the massacre," David explained, "Magua and some other Hurons seized Cora and Alice. They carried them away, and I insisted they take me, as well. Instead of killing us, they brought us all up here. They separated the ladies. Alice is being kept in a nearby Huron village. Cora was taken to a nearby village of the Delaware tribe."

"Indians do that sometimes," Hawkeye told Duncan. "They let another tribe hold on to some of their prisoners. It makes rescuing them all the more difficult."

"Why are you allowed to roam free?" Duncan asked David.

"As we were hiking north," David said, pushing his spectacles up on his nose, "I sang my psalms out of fear. The first time I did so, the Hurons looked at me with a kind of respect. When we got to the Huron village, they told me I could roam as I pleased—as long as I took on an Indian appearance."

"When David sing," Chingachgook explained in English, "Hurons think he be crazy in head. All Indian tribes treat crazy man with respect. They leave him be."

"So your singing came in very handy, after all," Hawkeye said, giving David a friendly nudge with his muzzle.

Uncas placed a hand on David's shoulder. "You no crazy, though. You brave man for staying by ladies."

"All right," Hawkeye said, digging at the ground with his paw. "So now we need to get Cora out of the Delaware village, and Alice out of the Huron village. Hmmm . . . let's see. Why don't I disguise myself and go back to the Huron village with David?"

Duncan looked at Hawkeye. "I should be the one to go. I can disguise myself more easily."

"What will you be disguised as?" Hawkeye asked playfully. "King Louis of France?"

"No, but you just gave me an idea," Duncan said

with a snap of his fingers. "I am not wearing my uniform. I can pass myself off as a French doctor of the woods. The Hurons are friendly with the French, and I speak the French language. Such a scheme could work."

Hawkeye nodded. Chingachgook pulled a small container from his pouch that held paint made from a mixture of plants and grease. He began applying paint designs to Duncan's face. Hawkeye knew that sometimes white men made use of Indian paint, and it would help to disguise Duncan. When Chingachgook was done, Duncan showed little resemblance to Major Duncan Heyward of the Sixtieth Regiment of the British army.

"Now, here's the plan," Hawkeye told Duncan. "You follow David back to the Huron village. The Mohicans and I will make our way toward the Delaware village and rescue Cora. Get Alice out of the village somehow. Then return here until we come for you."

Duncan nodded, then followed David through the tangled forest. As Hawkeye waved away an insect, he wondered if he would ever see the two of them again.

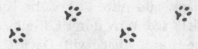

After a two-mile hike, Major Duncan Heyward followed David Gamut into the Huron village. Scattered around the village were about fifty small lodges. They were rough structures built from a patchwork of logs, bark, branches, and dirt. Most of the Hurons had settled in for the night, but Duncan noticed a few of them roaming the grounds, doing various chores.

A suspicious Huron warrior approached Duncan and escorted him into one of the lodges. Several Huron chiefs were seated around a blazing torch. Duncan explained in French that he was a doctor traveling to the French Fort Carillon.

The Hurons spoke some French. After much questioning, they believed the story. Not only that, but they also wanted Duncan to see if he could heal a Huron woman who had become very ill. Duncan had no choice but to agree to try.

Just then, an Indian prisoner was dragged into the hut. One of the Hurons told Duncan that the Indian had just been captured. He was to be tortured and killed at dawn.

When the prisoner came near the bright light of the torch, Duncan was horrified to see the youthful face of Uncas. The Mohican shot Duncan a warning look that said, *Say nothing about knowing me.*

Then several Hurons escorted Duncan through the village, and through an opening in the side of a mountain. Duncan followed the Hurons into a winding cave with many chambers. The major could see this was where the Hurons stored their food supply and valuable items.

Eventually, Duncan was left alone in a chamber where a sick woman lay on the ground, covered by a blanket. She was placed there so the evil spirits inside her would not infect the rest of the village.

Duncan knelt beside the woman, who was unconscious. Sensing the approach of something, Duncan turned around. He froze with fear, seeing that a black bear had wandered into the chamber. The beast's mouth was partly open, revealing a set of incredibly sharp teeth.

"Do not harm me," Duncan said in a soothing voice.

Suddenly, the bear did a starting thing. It rose to its hind legs, lifted its furry paws, and pulled off its head. The next thing Duncan knew, he was staring into the rugged face of—Hawkeye!

"What . . . how . . . why . . ." Duncan stammered.

Duncan looked so completely confused that Hawkeye couldn't stop himself from laughing for several minutes. Finally, the scout settled down enough to explain things.

"On the way to the Delaware village, Uncas felt the need to creep close to the Huron village to make sure you were all right. He crept a bit *too* close, and some Huron warriors captured him. I knew they would kill him. So I told Chingachgook to wait by the beaver pond while I went to rescue Uncas."

"I see," Duncan said slowly. "However, this still does not explain why you are . . . dressed as a bear."

"Well, I knew I'd need a good disguise," Hawkeye said, feeling the rough bear fur scratch against his own soft fur. "As luck would have it, I saw a French fur trader go by, carrying a complete bear skin. I talked him into lending me the skin. I cleaned it out a bit, cut some slits to see through, and then I stripped myself bare and put on the bear." Hawkeye chuckled at the play on words.

"Hawkeye, you're an odd one," remarked Duncan. "Nevertheless, we have friends to rescue. I still have not yet managed to find where Alice is being kept."

Hawkeye lifted his nose into the air and sniffed. "I believe I have. Follow me."

Hawkeye pulled the bear head back on top of his own furred head. Such moves were not easy to do. *Eight paws aren't necessarily better than four,* Hawkeye thought.

As Duncan followed, Hawkeye walked through the cave. Soon the men entered another chamber. Golden-haired Alice lay asleep on a blanket there. No one was around to guard her. Alice's dress was torn and dirty; otherwise, she appeared to be in fine shape.

As Duncan went about untying some straps that bound Alice at the hands and feet, he said, "Alice, wake up. I have come for you, my darling."

Eyes not fully opened, Alice murmured, "Oh, Duncan, is that you? You are a knight in shining armor having come to my rescue."

"Alice, we must leave quickly," Hawkeye said, as he nudged Alice with his bear muzzle.

Alice sat up, opening her beautiful blue eyes. She glanced at the painted face of Duncan. She stared at the ferocious face of the bear. Her eyes went wide with terror as she slumped to the ground, fainting dead away.

"No, Alice," Duncan whispered, "do not faint. It's me—Duncan. And this bear beside me is really—"

Duncan and Hawkeye both sensed someone behind them—they both turned.

The mean-looking figure of Magua stood at the chamber's entrance. "You are not a French doctor," Magua said, glaring at Duncan. "Major Heyward, you will watch woman die. Then you will die!"

Magua yanked his knife out of his belt. But Hawkeye lunged at Magua and held him down with two of his bear paws. While Magua struggled to pull away, Duncan seized Alice's binding and used it to tie Magua's hands and feet. Hawkeye pulled off his bear head.

"Agh!" Magua cried out upon seeing Hawkeye's face.

"Seems you don't have much to say," Hawkeye said, spearing a rag with one of his bear claws. He tied

the rag around Magua's mouth to prevent the Indian from calling for help.

"Throw the blanket around Alice and pick her up," Hawkeye said, as he slipped the bear head back on. "If a Huron tries to stop you, pretend Alice is that old woman you were supposed to heal. I'm afraid the sick Huron woman won't be rising anytime soon. Say you must take her into the woods to search for the proper plant roots to use as medicine. Then wait for me at the beaver pond. Let's go. We must reach the pond before they find Magua."

Duncan nodded. Then he carried Alice's limp body out of the cave. After a few moments, Hawkeye stumbled out of the cave. A few Hurons saw him but paid no attention. Hawkeye knew Indians felt comfortable around bears. They knew a bear would not attack them unless given a good reason to do so.

Soon Hawkeye wandered over to David Gamut, who was singing softly to himself and playing his pitch pipe beneath a tree. David gave the bear a nervous glance, but continued with his song. It was the psalm he had sung the night Hawkeye had first met him.

> *How good it is, O see,*
> *And how it pleaseth well . . .*

Hawkeye could not resist having a little fun. Through his big black bear head, he joined David on the words:

Together, e'en in unity,
For brethren so to dwell.

David's mouth fell open with amazement, and his pitch pipe slipped through his fingers.

"Hey, bears like to sing, too," Hawkeye said in a deep, growling voice. "Myself, I'm a bear-a-tone."

David could barely speak. "Oh, mysterious monster . . . can . . . can . . . such things be?"

His shaggy outer fur shaking with laughter, Hawkeye pulled off his bear head. David stared at the face of Hawkeye. The psalm-singer looked as if he might topple over.

"No, don't *you* faint, too," Hawkeye said, as he put the bear head back on. "I'll explain everything later. Right now, take me to Uncas."

David picked up his pitch pipe. Then he led Hawkeye to the lodge where Uncas was being held prisoner. Hawkeye continued his bear act as he entered the hut, in case any Hurons were present. Fortunately, there was no one around except for the young Uncas. He was bound by his hands and feet to a stake in the ground.

Desiring a last bit of fun, Hawkeye gave Uncas a bearish growl.

Uncas studied the bear a moment, then whispered, "Hawkeye?"

Hawkeye pulled off the bear head with annoyance. "Now, how did you know it was me, boy?"

"You not make good bear," Uncas said in his broken English.

"What do you mean, I don't make a good bear?" Hawkeye said, feeling offended. "I would like to see you do it better!"

"If you give me skin," Uncas replied with a smile, "I do better."

"Gentlemen, please," David interrupted. "Could we perhaps discuss this another time? If the Hurons find us like this, they will not be overly amused."

"You're right," Hawkeye said, beginning to dig at the ground with a bear paw. "David, untie Uncas while I think of a plan of escape. Hoot, it's getting hot in this outfit."

"Why not we run away?" Uncas suggested, as David went about unbinding his hands and feet.

"It's too risky," Hawkeye answered. "But, Uncas, you just gave me a good idea. Since you think you can play a bear so well, you'll put on the bear costume and do just that. If you're convincing, you can just walk on out of the village."

"No work Hawkeye. They capture you," Uncas pointed out.

"No, they won't," Hawkeye said with a sly grin. "Because I'm going to put on David's outfit and pretend I'm him. I know David's taller than I am, but from a distance the Hurons might fall for it. Then I, too, can walk out of the village."

"Uh . . . well . . ." David said, scratching his shaved head with confusion. "What about me?"

"You're going to play the part of Uncas," Hawkeye announced, proud of his clever plan.

David adjusted his spectacles. "But that is not

such a good part. Uncas is scheduled to be tortured and killed."

"Sorry," Hawkeye said with a shrug of his bear paws. "Not everyone gets the part they want. But I think it might work all right. When they discover who you really are, just start singing. They should leave you alone on account of your being crazy. And, listen, when you get free, head west. Keep sending out that snake signal you heard me make a while ago."

"Uh . . . very well," David said nervously. "I will do it."

"That's the spirit!" Hawkeye said, giving David a quick nudge with his muzzle. "Now, on the count of three, everyone take off their clothes!"

In a matter of minutes, the exchanging of outfits was completed. David lay on the floor of the hut, tied up and dressed as Uncas. After wishing David good luck, Hawkeye walked out of the hut wearing David's clothing. As he walked along calmly, he sang a few lines of a psalm. After a ways, he looked back to see Uncas moving heavily across the ground on all fours, wearing the bear costume.

A few Hurons turned to watch the singer and the bear, but no one stopped them from leaving the village.

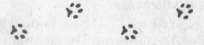

As the first pink of dawn tinted the sky, twenty Hurons moved in single file through the forest. Leading them was Magua, who wore an angry scowl. As the

Hurons approached the beaver pond, some of them turned to see an especially large beaver watching them curiously from inside one of the mud huts.

The Hurons continued on their way, heading in the direction of the Delaware village. When the Hurons passed out of sight, the large beaver removed his head—revealing the bronzed face of Chingachgook.

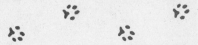

Hawkeye has just sneaked inside of enemy territory.

In the meantime, I'm about to enter the enemy territory of Mr. King's office.

Hawkeye was disguised as a bear.

I think that I'm going to need to pretend I'm something I'm not, as well. How about . . . Oh, I know.

Chapter Eleven

As elevator doors slid open, Wishbone stepped into the offices of King Development Corporation. The dog had gone there to see if he could find the pages that he and his friends suspected Mr. King had torn from the library books.

Now, just pretend you're a respectable businessman, Wishbone reminded himself, as he walked through an elegant waiting room.

Wishbone trotted over to a circular desk. A very businesslike receptionist sat there, writing something in an appointment book.

Deepening his voice, Wishbone said, "Excuse me, ma'am."

The woman didn't seem to hear Wishbone. The dog raised himself up onto his hind legs and placed his front paws on the desk. Finally, she looked over the front edge of the desk. She wrinkled her eyebrows when she saw Wishbone. "Oh, my goodness. How did you get in here?"

"I took the elevator," Wishbone said in his most

businesslike manner. "My name is . . . uh . . . Wisher. Walter Wisher. I'm with International Bone Management—I'm here to see Leon King. He and I have a business deal we're chewing on together."

With a frown, the receptionist turned to another lady who was passing by. "Sarah, there's a dog at my desk. Do you know who brought it in here?"

Sarah crouched down to pet the top of Wishbone's head.

"No, I don't, Miss Hardcastle. . . . Oh, what a cute little doggie."

"Excuse me," Wishbone said, trying to keep the situation businesslike. "I know Mr. King isn't here right now. My appointment isn't until one o'clock. If it's all right with you, I'll just let myself into his office. You don't need to show me the way. I can just follow his scent."

Wishbone strolled past the reception desk. He entered a large space where a number of people were at work in cubicles. Miss Hardcastle came running after Wishbone. "No, no, no!" she called. "I'm afraid you have to leave. We can't have animals around here."

Wishbone shot the woman an annoyed look. "Listen, lady, I've been working my tail off all morning, and I don't have time for this nonsense. Mr. King would be very unhappy if he knew you were treating me as if I were just some mutt who wandered in off the street."

By now the people in the cubicles were watching the scene with amusement. Miss Hardcastle, however, did not look the least bit amused. She hurried over to Wishbone and picked him up rather roughly.

"Hey! Handle with care!" Wishbone called out. "This is canine harassment!"

"No dogs allowed," Miss Hardcastle scolded as she carried Wishbone away.

This is totally *undignified,* Wishbone thought, as several people in the area laughed. *And I really need to get into Mr. King's office. I'm pretty sure that's where he put the pages that he tore out of those books. What I need to do now is create a bit of confusion. Here goes nothing!*

Wishbone leaped out of Miss Hardcastle's arms and began to run wildly around the room. He leaped over a box of paper, knocked down a wastebasket, and ran under a desk and out the other side.

"Catch the dog!" Miss Hardcastle yelled at the top of her lungs.

"Where is he?" someone called, while crawling on the floor.

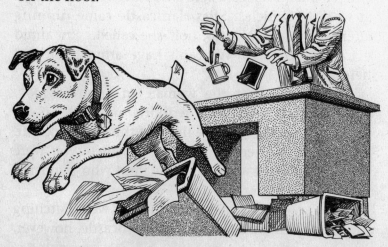

"People, I cannot work in this environment!" someone else exclaimed, throwing down a pen in frustration.

Wishbone went to a cord plugged into the wall and yanked it out with his teeth.

"Hey! Someone killed the power on my computer!" a worker cried out with panic. "It must have been that crazy dog!"

By now there was so much confusion in the room that no one noticed Wishbone moving to a door where Leon King's scent was the strongest. Wishbone nudged open the door with his muzzle, entered, then nudged the door shut.

The large office was elegantly decorated with leather furniture and colorful paintings that looked a lot like Mr. King's ties. Wishbone jumped up into a swivel chair that sat by a big wooden desk.

He put his front paws on the desk and looked around. *Now, where could those missing pages be? When I have something I don't want anyone to get his paws on, what do I do with it? Of course, I bury it. That carpet looks really tough to dig through, though. Where else . . . I know!*

Wishbone worked open the top desk drawer with his muzzle. After pawing through a collection of papers and office supplies, he found three sheets of paper, each with a ragged edge. The dog's tail went wagging. He could tell at once that these were the pages torn from the library books.

Hearing footsteps approaching the office, Wishbone crumpled one of the pages and held it inside his mouth. As soon as the paper was out of sight, the door flew open.

Miss Hardcastle stood there, scowling as if she had just swallowed a box of staples. She shook a finger at Wishbone, saying, "You are a very naughty dog. I'm very tempted to call the town dogcatcher!"

Wishbone leaped off the chair and ran through Miss Hardcastle's legs.

"There he goes!" Miss Hardcastle screamed as she ran after the dog. "Somebody stop that awful dog!"

As people flew left and right, Wishbone escaped past the cubicles and reception desk. Just then, the elevator doors slid open. A delivery man stepped out, carrying a package. Wishbone stepped inside the elevator and watched the doors close just as Miss Hardcastle came rushing wildly toward him.

Now, Wishbone thought with relief, *I just need to reach that lobby button again.*

I bet you're eager to know what was printed on that page I grabbed. You'll find out soon enough. But right now I need to head over to city hall for that decision about building on the park land.

On the way, maybe we should make a quick stop in the Delaware village to hear another kind of decision.

Chapter Twelve

A warm sun rose over the Delaware village, which looked much like the Huron village. Hawkeye sat outside a lodge, scratching at his fur as he watched the morning activities. The Delaware women were busy preparing the breakfast meal. The Delaware men sat around, examining and cleaning their weapons. Nearby, a group of Delaware children played a stick-tossing game that looked rather fun to the scout.

Hawkeye, Duncan, Alice, and Uncas had arrived in the village late the previous night. The scout knew some of the Delawares and was received there in a friendly manner. He sat on the ground beside Duncan, Uncas, Alice, and Cora.

Cora had been with the Delawares the past few days, and they had treated her well. Her dark hair was a bit wilder than before, but the scout thought she looked lovelier than ever. The Delawares were friendly to their guests. Even so, a few Delaware men sat nearby, making sure Cora did not attempt to escape. The Delawares had promised Magua they would hold on to Cora, and most Indians were very good about keeping their promises.

I think I may have picked up a few forest fleas, Hawkeye thought as he scratched. *Ah, they won't kill me. By the way, I wonder what happened to David Gamut. And I wonder where Chingachgook is hiding out. I also wonder how long Magua stayed tied up in the . . . Ah, speak of the devil, here comes the villain now.*

About twenty Huron warriors came marching into the village. They were led by Magua, who wore a terrible scowl on his face. Hawkeye could see right away that Magua had become the leader of the Huron warriors. Alice gasped with fear. Major Heyward, who by now had cleaned his face of the paint, took her hand.

Now I've got something worse than fleas to worry about, Hawkeye thought as his eyes met those of Magua.

Everyone in the village dropped what they were doing and came to sit in a wide circle around the visitors. When a Delaware chief approached Magua, the evil Huron took on the dignified manner of the chief he hoped to be. Hawkeye lifted his ears as Magua spoke to the Delaware chief in the Delaware language, which Hawkeye understood fairly well.

"I have come for my rightful prisoners," Magua announced. "The maid with the dark hair. The maid with the yellow hair. And the young Mohican."

"We have promised to keep the dark-haired maid for you," the Delaware chief told Magua. "I do not know about the others. This a matter to be decided by our great leader."

As the chief went to a lodge, Cora whispered to Hawkeye, "Will they allow Magua to take us?"

"I don't know," Hawkeye whispered, shaking some dust off his tail. "On the one hand, the Delawares are friendly with the Hurons because they are both allies of the French. On the other hand, the Delawares and Hurons sometimes fight over the land around here. On the third hand, the Delawares might be sympathetic to Uncas, because the Delawares and the Mohicans originally came from the same family. But we'll know soon enough. The Delaware leader will now conduct a sort of court trial. And, while we are on Delaware ground, we must go along with his ruling."

A few minutes later, a man almost a century in age appeared from a lodge. He moved along very slowly, assisted by a young boy. His body was bent, his bronzed face covered with as many wrinkles as weathered tree bark. Three feathers were tied into his snowy-white hair, which fell all the way to his shoulders.

Soon the boy helped the man onto a wooden platform. There he lowered himself into a seat. Hawkeye knew this was the famous Tamenund, the wisest and oldest Indian chief in the region.

Magua made a gesture of respect to Tamenund, then spoke the language of the Delawares. "Wise Father, these people I ask for are my rightful prisoners. As you know, the men of red skin must act as brothers, even though we be of different tribes. It is the only way we will overcome the white men who attempt to steal all our gifts of woods and waters."

Tamenund closed his eyes, as if drifting deep into memory. "What you say is true," he said in a raspy voice. "When I was a laughing boy, one day I stood upon the seashore. Out of the sun, I see a big boat coming. Sails fly over the boat like the wings of a white swan. This was my first sight of the white man. It seems like only yesterday. But now the white men are as many as the leaves on the trees. They move through every part of the woods, fighting to see who will own all this land. Before my sun sets, I hope to see them disappear."

Hawkeye gave his fur a concerned scratch.

A smile played on Magua's lips. "Wise Father who has lived many days, I am glad you see things my way."

"What will you do with these prisoners?" asked Tamenund.

"The maidens with dark and yellow hair," Magua explained, "I may allow to live in my village. The young Mohican I will kill. He is a false red man. His tribe has almost vanished, yet he does not live with another tribe. He lives with the white man who sits over there. Together they kill many red men."

A murmur moved through the crowd of people watching the scene. Tamenund sat motionless, listening to all Magua had to say.

"I also ask permission to kill the two white men," Magua continued. "One is an officer in the British army, an enemy to our French allies. The other is a man known as Hawkeye. He has killed so many red men that he can no longer count the number."

Several of the Delaware warriors leaped to their feet. They pulled out knives that gleamed in the morning sun. Hawkeye licked a paw casually to show the warriors he was not afraid.

Tamenund fixed his aged eyes on Uncas. "Mohican, are you as false as this Huron claims?"

Uncas rose to his feet and walked proudly over to Tamenund. He opened the front of his hunting shirt, revealing on his chest the blue tattoo of a turtle. "Wise Father," Uncas said in the Delaware language, "I am no false red man. I come from the turtle clan of the Mohican tribe. I am Uncas, son of Chingachgook, who is son of Uncas before me. Now all my tribe have returned to the earth, except for my father and I."

Tamenund studied Uncas a moment, then closed his eyes. "Ah, yes, I knew your grandfather. He was a very brave and wise man. I have heard say his son, Chingachgook, is his father's equal. Because you come from the same blood as these men, I doubt you to be a false red man. I believe you may grow to be one of the great leaders of the red people."

Uncas pointed toward Duncan and Hawkeye. "The British officer and the white man known as Hawkeye are good men. They wish no harm to the Delawares."

Tamenund opened his eyes. "Then they will live. But are you, Uncas, the rightful prisoner of this Huron?"

"I *was* his rightful prisoner," Uncas said, "but I

escaped. This means I am no longer his rightful prisoner. Same is true of the maiden with yellow hair."

"Then the Huron shall not take Uncas or the maiden with the yellow hair," Tamenund declared.

As Hawkeye shifted to scratch a spot, he saw Magua's nostrils flare, like those of an angry tiger.

"Then give me only the maiden with the dark hair," Magua said, taking a step toward Tamenund. "She has *not* rightfully escaped. I gave her into the keeping of the Delawares, and here she has stayed. She is rightfully mine!"

"Is this true?" Tamenund asked Uncas.

Uncas glanced sadly at the ground. "Yes, it is so."

Tamenund gave a solemn nod. "Then the Huron may take the maiden with the dark hair. I have no other choice."

Flashing a smile of triumph, Magua walked over to where Cora sat. He reached out a hand to her, saying in English, "You come with me now."

"No!" Alice screamed, clutching at her sister.

"It's all right," Cora said, rising calmly to her feet. "I will go. I want no blood shed over me."

Magua wrapped his hand around Cora's wrist, then got ready to leave with her. Because this was like a court situation, Hawkeye knew it would be most improper for him to attack Magua in this place. But he felt the need to do something.

The scout sprang to all fours and called out in English, "Hey, Magua, hold on a second there."

Magua looked down at Hawkeye with a sneer. "What have you to say, white man?"

"Well," Hawkeye said in his friendliest manner, "I have an honest deal to offer you. If you set that woman free, you can take me in her place. You can kill me, or you can keep me tied up as your prisoner. And, believe me, I hate being tied up. I figure you'll choose to kill me, though."

Shocked whispers went around the village.

"You will give your own life for the life of the woman?" Magua asked with disbelief.

All eyes turned to the scout, who dug at the ground bashfully with his paw. "I suppose every man has to die sooner or later. Right now is a little sooner than I would have liked, but so be it. If I had a wife or children, I might think differently. But as it is, there's no one much to mourn me—except for my good friends, Chingachgook and Uncas."

"I know several others who will mourn for you," Duncan said quietly.

"You are brave man," Magua told Hawkeye with a hint of admiration.

"In your way, so are you," Hawkeye told Magua.

Magua's face seemed to freeze into a sheet of ice. "Still, I refuse the offer. I take the woman!"

Hawkeye felt his tail droop with disappointment. Tamenund had ruled that Magua had a right to take the prisoner. The scout knew there was nothing more he or anyone else could do to save Cora Munro—at least not in the Delaware village.

Cora knelt down to Hawkeye and ran a hand over his furred back. "Hawkeye, your heart is as large as this country around us. I shall never forget you."

Hawkeye said, "Thank you for the kind words, ma'am."

Cora embraced Duncan, then gave Alice a kiss on the cheek. "Duncan, be a good and loving husband to my dear sister. Alice, I will think of you no matter where I go."

Lastly, Cora walked over to Uncas and held the young Mohican with her steady eyes. Hawkeye could see that a deep love had formed between these two, even though it had never been expressed with words. Cora placed her hand on Uncas's bronzed chest, right over the turtle. Uncas placed his hand over Cora's hand. After a few tender moments in this position, Cora wiped a tear from her eye. Then the two broke their touch, and Cora walked over to the waiting Magua.

"Magua!" Uncas called out in a fierce voice. "Look at the sun. It is now rising above the branches. While on Delaware ground, you have a right to take your prisoner. But when you leave this ground, I have a right to win her back. When the sun burns high above the trees, I shall be on your trail!"

Magua glared hatefully at Uncas, then spread his glare around the entire village. In a chilling voice, he cried out, "All of you here are but crows. And I spit on you!"

Magua grabbed Cora roughly by the arm and pulled her away. The Huron warriors followed, keeping their hands on their weapons. None of the Delawares moved a muscle.

Uncas kept his eyes on Cora until the colors of her

dress blended into the forest foliage. Then Uncas walked with a determined step and disappeared inside one of the lodges.

The Delaware people began buzzing like a hive of bees, discussing the drama they had witnessed. Aided by the boy, Tamenund made his way slowly back to his lodge.

While Duncan held the weeping Alice in his arms, Hawkeye chewed on a wooden spoon one of the women had used to prepare the tribe's breakfast. He had a good idea of what Uncas was up to.

After some time, Uncas stepped out of the lodge. He had removed his shirt and painted deep red and yellow stripes across his face. Hawkeye knew that was a design of war.

Uncas walked to a wooden post that stood in the center of the village. He began to move around it with a rhythmic dancelike step, all the while chanting. At first Uncas murmured in low tones. Then his voice gradually raised in pitch and volume until he was screaming with an animal wildness.

Hawkeye knew Uncas was performing a war dance, in which he asked the Great Spirit to watch over him in the coming battle.

One by one, the Delaware warriors joined Uncas, dancing and chanting around the post. Soon many warriors were performing the war dance, which grew into a state of frightful frenzy. The sound of their chant became so alarming that it made the fur on Hawkeye's back creep upward.

"What is happening?" Duncan whispered to Hawkeye.

Hawkeye stopped chewing on the wooden spoon. "Uncas is going after Cora, and the Delawares have decided to join Uncas in his quest. I'm not much for singing and dancing myself, but I reckon I, too, will be joining the fight."

"As will I," Duncan said, keeping an arm around Alice.

With a ferocious shout, Uncas pulled his tomahawk from his belt and hurled it across the village. The blade sliced into a tree, sending a piece of bark falling to the ground.

Hawkeye lifted his muzzle to see that the sun was now almost directly above the trees.

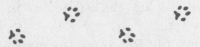

It's nearing high noon, which means it's about time for the big showdown with Magua.

And let's not forget that my friends and I have a showdown coming up with Mr. King at the Oakdale City Hall. Come on! We're late!

Chapter Thirteen

Joe glanced at the clock on the wall. It was already five minutes past noon. He tapped his fingers nervously on his leg. He was seated in the meeting room of City Hall.

At the front of the room, the mayor and the four town council members sat behind a large, curved desk. Several rows of seats occupied the rest of the room. Citizens were always welcome to attend the open hearings that dealt with town affairs.

Joe, Sam, David, and Mr. Bloodgood sat on one side of the front row. Mr. King sat on the other side of the same row. The only other people present were the two surveyors Joe had seen in the park that morning. They stood at a podium, explaining the findings of their measurements.

The mayor sat at the center of the desk. "Let me try to understand this very clearly," the mayor said to the surveyors. "According to your measurements, Mr. King is correct in assuming that he owns the land in question."

"Yes, sir," one of the surveyors answered.

The mayor looked at Mr. King. "It is unfortunate that the land we thought fell within the boundaries of Jackson Park is actually private property. However, this being the case, and since you are the owner, the town council has no legal right to prevent you from building on this land."

Mr. King smoothed his tie as he stood. "I assure you, Mr. Mayor, my restaurant will be good for the town's economic development . . . not to mention my *own* economic development. When I open this Tastee Oasis, I would like to treat you and each of the fine town council members to a free meal."

The mayor prepared to bang a gavel on the desk. Such an action would indicate the situation had been resolved.

Mr. Bloodgood rose to his feet. "Excuse me, Mr. Mayor. I have something that I'd like to say on the matter of Mr. King's property."

"Very well," the mayor said, setting down the gavel. "We believe in hearing all opinions in this room."

As Mr. Bloodgood moved to the podium, Mr. King sat down with an irritated sigh. Joe crossed his fingers, noticing that Sam and David did the same. This was their last chance.

Mr. Bloodgood cleared his throat, then spoke. "It *seems* Mr. King has the legal right to that property. But things are not always what they seem. I urge you to hold off on your decision until the matter has been researched in more depth. I suspect Mr. King may not have been completely honest in this deal. There is reason to suspect that he once knocked down some signs announcing a town council hearing. This happened the last time he tried to build his Tastee Oasis."

"I never did any such thing!" Mr. King called out, as if he was greatly offended.

"Maybe you didn't," Mr. Bloodgood said calmly. "But, on the other hand, maybe you did. The point is, such trickery has been used in land deals before. Ask the Chippewa, or the Seneca, or the Cherokees, or the Sioux, or the Apache—or any of this country's Native American tribes. Much of their land was taken away by violence. But even more of it was stolen by underhanded legal shenanigans. We Native Americans call it 'speaking with a false tongue.' This land is not considered Native American property, but I think I speak for most of the citizens of Oakdale when I say our parks are very important to us."

"This man," Mr. King said with a sneer, "is talking about Indian tribes that lost their land over a hundred years ago. This lecture has no relation at all to what we are discussing now."

"Perhaps," the mayor said, twirling his gavel in his hand. "But I will allow Mr. Bloodgood to finish his remarks."

Joe crossed his fingers more tightly.

"Mr. Mayor," Mr. Bloodgood said, gripping both sides of the podium, "I think America is a great country. Maybe the greatest anywhere. But if we have one weakness in this land, it is the weakness of greed. And greed makes people do underhanded things."

"I don't believe this!" Mr. King grumbled.

Mr. Bloodgood glared at Mr. King. Then he continued his speech. "When the white settlers colonized the eastern part of this country, they made the Native Americans leave. But they promised the Native Americans that they could have all the land west of the Mississippi River. However, the settlers soon changed their minds. They used all sorts of legal schemes to seize that land, too.

"Before long, the rolling trains had replaced the running buffalo. Native Americans were forced to live on little patches of land called reservations.

"Now many people in this country are ashamed of what happened to the Native Americans. Many folks in this town may also end up feeling ashamed if we foolishly give away part of Jackson Park. All I am saying is, let us examine the situation more fully before a final decision is made about what is to be done. Remember, once a tree is chopped down, it can never be brought back to life."

Joe noticed that the mayor and town council members looked very moved by Mr. Bloodgood's plea. Joe held his breath, waiting for the answer. David and Sam stared straight ahead with tense expressions.

"Mr. Bloodgood, your words are well spoken," the mayor told him. "Nevertheless . . . it seems clear that the land in question is the rightful property of Mr. King. I don't like the situation any more than you do. But the law is the law."

Mr. King leaned back in his seat, chuckling.

Mr. Bloodgood bowed his head with disappointment.

Feeling something rub against his leg, Joe looked down. He was surprised to see Wishbone, who had made his way into the room without anyone noticing. The dog held a crumpled piece of paper in his mouth.

Joe quickly took Wishbone back to the second row of seats so the dog would not be seen by anybody else in the room. "Wishbone," he whispered, "you're not supposed to be here."

With his muzzle, Wishbone held out the piece of paper to his pal.

Joe pulled the paper from the dog's mouth and looked at it in confusion. Noticing Wishbone, Sam and David joined Joe in the second row.

"Hey!" Sam said, leaning in to examine the paper. "It looks like a page torn out of one of the copies of the book about Oakdale's history. I wonder where Wishbone found it."

As the mayor said a few last words, Joe, Sam, and David read over the page. At almost the same moment, all of their eyes jumped wide with surprise.

"Tell the mayor about this," Wishbone urged the kids. "I would do it myself, but I think I should stay out of sight."

"Mr. Mayor, just a minute, please!" Joe called out with excitement. He rushed to the podium to show Mr. Bloodgood the page. As Joe returned to his seat, he noticed Mr. King nervously chewing his lip. Everyone waited while Mr. Bloodgood read over the information.

Finally, Mr. Bloodgood set down the page, a slight smile on his lips. "Mr. Mayor, I believe I have discovered Mr. King's little trick. As the surveyors explained, the deed indicates that the boundary measurements for Jackson Park are to be taken off the fixed point of the old post office building."

"Yes, we know that," the mayor said, growing impatient. "According to those measurements, the land Mr. King has purchased does not fall in the park's legal boundaries."

"True," Mr. Bloodgood said, lifting the crumpled page. "But I hold here a page from a book titled *Oakdale— A Little Town with a Big History.* This page states that in 1927 the town council considered tearing down the old post office to make way for some new buildings.

However, the council decided not to tear it down because it was such an important part of the town's history. Instead, the council voted to *move* the old post office. Yes—move it twenty yards toward the end of Oak Street."

All of the town council members looked surprised. "Oh," the mayor said, raising his eyebrows. "I didn't know that. But I'm sure we can check it in the town records."

Mr. Bloodgood glanced at a scowling Mr. King, then continued. "What this means is that those measurements made today are incorrect. The measurements were taken off the *new* location of the old post office. They *should* have been taken off the *old* location of the old post office."

"In other words," Wishbone whispered to the three kids, "Mr. King's *new* Tastee Oasis is now *old* history."

One of the surveyors stepped forward. "Mr. Bloodgood is right. If that landmark was moved twenty yards from its original location, that would throw all the measurements way off. Even if it was moved two feet, it would throw them off."

"I see," the mayor said with a pleased expression. He turned to Mr. King. "Obviously, Mr. King, you were aware of this information and used it to your advantage, even though you must have known that your actions were dishonest." The mayor then looked directly at Mr. Bloodgood. "Mr. Bloodgood, very good investigative work!"

Mr. Bloodgood pointed at Joe, Sam, and David. "It

wasn't me. These young friends of mine figured it out. Maybe they will explain in more detail."

"Well, it was mostly me," Wishbone muttered from his hiding place behind the front-row seats.

Joe stood and told the story of what he and his friends had done that day. He mentioned seeing Mr. King at the library. He also spoke about the torn pages from the library books.

Wishbone thought about coming forward to tell how he found the missing pages in Mr. King's office, but he decided to keep quiet. He realized he might get thrown in the dog pound for trespassing.

When Joe was done, the mayor and the four council members had a quiet discussion among themselves.

Mr. King turned to the kids angrily. "How did you get that page?"

Sam looked at Mr. King calmly. "We have our sources," she said, smiling.

"If one of you broke into my office," Mr. King said, pointing a threatening finger, "that is theft!"

David looked pleased. "So you admit this torn page came from your office. That suggests you were the one who tore it!"

"No, I didn't say that!" Mr. King said, raising his voice.

The mayor raised a hand for silence. "My fellow council members and I—"

"Mr. Mayor, listen," Mr. King said, rising to his feet with a big smile. "Even if some of this is true, that does not change the wording of—"

"Mr. King, keep still," the mayor said sharply. "My fellow council members and I have decided *not* to approve your right to the property in question for the moment. We will have the town records checked. If they show this new information to be accurate, the surveyors will remeasure the land based on the old post office's *old* location. I have a hunch these new measurements will show that you have no right to this land."

Mr. King dropped his smile. "What? You can't do that! You can't rob me of a business deal worth a bundle of money because of some little technicality!"

The mayor pointed his gavel at Mr. King. "I can—and I will. And I'm about to remove some more of your money. I hereby fine you a sum of two hundred dollars for tearing up valuable library books!"

The mayor pounded his gavel on the desk.

Mr. King stomped out of the room, his shiny black shoes smacking against the tile floor. Everyone applauded the mayor's decision, while Wishbone wagged his tail triumphantly.

Hip-hip, hooray! Victory for me! I helped save the park!

Now, let's see if Hawkeye can help save Cora. Don't forget, she's still in the dangerous hands of Magua.

Chapter Fourteen

With ears bent back and body low to the ground, Hawkeye moved silently through the woods. Major Duncan Heyward and twenty Delaware warriors crept behind him. They moved in single file. Each man stepped in Hawkeye's prints so an enemy spy would not be able to guess how many had traveled this way.

Young Uncas and seven Delaware chiefs led groups of a similar size some distance away. In all, there were almost two hundred Delaware warriors following Magua.

Dark clouds drifted across the sky, as if warning the entire forest that this was to be a day of doom. Raising his ears high, Hawkeye heard many things— birds fluttering in tree branches, a squirrel dropping a nut, a bug inching along a leaf. But, so far, he heard no sign of the enemy Hurons.

After creeping another quarter-mile, Hawkeye heard footsteps up ahead crunching hurriedly over twigs. Through the trees, he saw an Indian running rather clumsily. Figuring it was a Huron, Hawkeye reached for his rifle. But then he saw a ray of sun glint off the Indian's spectacles.

There's only one red man who wears those things, Hawkeye thought, as he signaled for his men to stop. The scout made a snakelike hissing sound. Upon hearing the signal, the Indian with spectacles shifted direction and came running to Hawkeye.

"Well, hello, there," Hawkeye greeted the psalm-singer. "I'm mighty glad to see you're still alive."

After catching his breath, David spoke. "When Magua finally got loose and discovered I wasn't Uncas, he raged like a wild wolf. I thought for certain he was going to kill me, so I began to sing a psalm. Even Magua respected my 'craziness' and allowed me to live. Then he gathered a group of warriors and stormed off toward the Delaware village."

"I saw him there," Hawkeye said, keeping a cautious eye on the surrounding woods.

"Just a little while ago," David continued, "Magua returned to the Huron village with Cora. Magua put her in the same cave where they had kept Alice. Then Magua left with several hundred warriors, all painted for battle. They wait halfway between this spot and the Huron village. I went out searching for you so I could give warning."

"I appreciate your effort," Hawkeye said, giving David a thankful pat with his paw. "You'd better stay here. I fear there's going to be some serious fighting this afternoon."

"I will join you in battle," David said as he pushed his spectacles up on his nose. "I see now the truth of your ways, Hawkeye. When evil walks the earth, some-times a man must fight."

"You're not a natural fighter," Hawkeye told him. "Besides, you don't even have a gun."

"I don't want a gun," David replied. "They frighten me with their loud bangs. However, I have made a weapon—the same weapon that was used by young David in the Bible." David pulled out a roughly made slingshot that he had created from sticks and vines.

Hawkeye couldn't help but chuckle. "I don't know how much good that thing will be against this Goliath of the Hurons. But, hoot, man, you're welcome to give it a try."

As David gathered some pebbles from a nearby brook, Uncas crept over to talk to Hawkeye. "I can hear Hurons up ahead," Uncas whispered in Mohican. "Let us charge them now."

Hawkeye began to draw a battle plan in the dirt with his paw. "No, boy, you are letting anger rob you of good judgment. Here is a better plan. I will take my men up near the beaver pond. When we get there, we will begin the whoop. That should draw most of the Hurons toward us. Then you and the rest of the Delawares will attack them from either side. We should be able to make our way toward the Huron village, where we can search for Cora. Is this plan good?"

Uncas nodded, his eyes set with determination.

As Uncas crept away, Hawkeye led his men slowly along the course of the trickling brook. After a mile, Hawkeye could see where the brook flowed into the beaver pond.

With ears raised high, Hawkeye listened carefully. He heard nothing except a light rustling of leaves. The scout knew the forest was far too quiet.

There's not a single Huron in sight, Hawkeye thought, as he took his rifle in his front paws. *But I know they are straight ahead, hiding, watching our every move. I can almost feel them breathing down on my fur.*

Hawkeye lifted a paw to his mouth and howled out the loudest whoop he could muster. As the Delawares joined in, the forest shook with the frightening Indian whoop of war.

Like a pack of panthers springing on their prey, at least two hundred Huron warriors leaped out of nowhere. Immediately, rifles on both sides began to fire.

Hawkeye glimpsed beavers fleeing through the pond, while the shots pattered among the leaves like raindrops. The scout couldn't resist a snort of humor when he saw David flinging pebble after pebble at the enemy with his crude slingshot.

Then a chorus of fresh whoops burst forth as Uncas and the rest of the Delawares charged at the Hurons from several directions. The shock of the attack allowed the Delawares to push the enemy back almost to the beaver pond.

Hawkeye rushed forward to a spot behind a tree. Duncan raced behind the same tree and began to reload his pistol. A bullet struck the bark, just inches from the scout's furred head.

"We could use a general like you in the British army," Duncan told Hawkeye.

"No, thanks," Hawkeye said, as he grabbed his powder horn with his teeth.

Suddenly a rifle cracked from right beside a beaver hut, behind the enemy. Many Hurons turned around, fearing another group was attacking from that direction. At first Hawkeye thought a beaver had volunteered to join the Delaware forces, but then he caught a glimpse of Chingachgook's brave face.

"It's my old friend, Chingachgook!" Hawkeye cried, his tail wagging with joy. "I was wondering where he was!"

"And he's giving our men a chance to advance even farther," Duncan noted.

Hawkeye's ears leaped up when he heard a voice cry, "Magua, you will not do it!" Hawkeye scanned the frantic battlefield to see Magua and two other Hurons racing their fastest toward the Huron village. They were being chased by a furious Uncas.

"Why is Uncas chasing Magua?" Duncan asked the scout.

"I fear the worst," Hawkeye replied. "Perhaps Magua senses defeat, and so he is rushing off to kill Cora!"

Hawkeye bounded after Magua, followed by Duncan and then David Gamut. With ears bouncing and paws pounding the ground, Hawkeye raced like the wind. The trees rushed by so fast they turned into a greenish blur, and soon the violent noises of the battle were far behind the scout's tail.

Magua and the two Hurons held a strong lead. But Uncas, Hawkeye, Duncan, and David stayed hard on their trail. Before long, the men were dashing through the many lodges of the Huron village. A group of Huron women ran over to block Hawkeye and his friends, but the scout unleashed a ferocious snarl to scare the women away. Up ahead, Hawkeye saw Magua and the Hurons round a corner and disappear into the same mountain cave where Alice had been held prisoner.

Rounding the corner, Hawkeye and his companions followed the Hurons into the cave. Hawkeye felt the rocky ground tear into his paws as he dashed through the cave's almost total darkness. The going got tougher, and Hawkeye realized the tunnel was actually sloping upward. Soon the scout's tongue was hanging out and he was aware of the loud sound of his panting.

After rounding a bend in the tunnel, Hawkeye could make out the distant figures of Magua and the Hurons. Through the darkness, Hawkeye caught sight of a woman's dress. He realized Magua was now dragging the dark-haired Cora with him.

"Cora!" Uncas cried out, his voice echoing loudly off the rocky walls. The Mohican threw down his rifle and, with superhuman effort, pressed ahead with even more speed.

Suddenly, Magua, Cora, the two Hurons, and then Uncas disappeared from view. After running a ways farther, Hawkeye pushed through a hole in the wall and found himself standing in daylight, high on a rocky mountainside.

When Hawkeye glanced down, his tail thumped with fright. The ground lay a dizzying distance below, at least a thousand feet. The gigantic trees appeared to be tiny plants. Amid the greenery, Hawkeye saw the Delawares and Hurons engaged in battle. Their bodies seemed to be the size of ants.

Duncan and David came out of the cave. Turning his muzzle upward, Hawkeye saw Magua, Cora, and the two Hurons standing on a rocky ledge a good distance overhead. But Uncas was nowhere to be seen. The upper portion of the mountain was very steep. Hawkeye realized it would take a great deal of effort for him and his friends to reach Cora. And, unfortunately, some scattered boulders would make it very easy for the Hurons to take cover and avoid being hit by flying bullets.

"We can't make it up there fast enough," Hawkeye said. "All we can do is try to bring them down with gunfire."

Hawkeye, Duncan, and David spread out on the mountainside. Each man readied his weapon. *I just don't have a clear enough shot at him,* Hawkeye thought, as he aimed his rifle at Magua. *And if I miss, it takes sooo long to reload these things.*

Hawkeye noticed that the upper half of Magua's face was covered with a mask of black war paint. Magua held his knife to Cora's throat. The Huron yelled in English, "Woman, choose! Either be my wife, or you die!"

Cora yanked herself free of Magua and knelt on the rock outcropping. "Oh, Lord!" she exclaimed. She clasped her hands in prayer. "I am thine. Do with me as thou seest best."

Magua's eyes burned like those of a demon as he

raised his knife to stab Cora. The blade swooped halfway down. Then, suddenly, Magua stopped. He gritted his teeth in agony.

At first Hawkeye thought Magua had been wounded. Then he realized the Huron was struggling only with himself. He obviously wanted to kill Cora, yet he could not quite bring himself to do so.

I still don't have a clear shot at him, Hawkeye thought, his tongue panting from the afternoon's heat. *And where in the world is Uncas?*

Major Duncan Heyward fired his pistol, but the shot zinged harmlessly off a rock. One of the Hurons hurled his tomahawk down at Duncan. The blade caught the major in the arm.

Crying out with pain, Duncan dropped his weapon. Hawkeye could see that Duncan was wounded by the tomahawk, but he was not seriously hurt.

Suddenly, the same Huron who had thrown the tomahawk fell to the ground. He had been struck on the forehead by a small object. He didn't seem dead, but at least he was out of action for the moment.

What do you know? Hawkeye thought, as he turned his muzzle to see David Gamut holding his slingshot. *He got one of them with that device. All right! That's one down, two remaining.*

Again Magua raised high his knife. His voice choking with anger, he screamed, "Woman, I have given you every chance. Now I kill you!"

From near the mountain's peak, a figure soared down like an eagle, landing on its feet beside Magua. This was Uncas, who held his knife out, ready to strike. Magua quickly backed away a few steps.

If Magua would take a few more steps, Hawkeye thought, easing his rifle to the right, *then I'd have a good shot.*

Then Hawkeye felt every fur on his back shoot up with panic. He yelped loudly, "Cora, watch out!"

It was too late. Before anyone could do anything, the other Huron on the rock had buried his knife in Cora's chest. Cora's eyes opened wide as she fell facedown on the rock. Hawkeye knew at once she was dead.

Sounding a shout of rage, Uncas yanked the murderer to his feet and jabbed his knife into the man's back. Then Uncas hurled the Huron to the ground, causing him to topple roughly down the mountainside.

Magua lunged his knife at Uncas, but Uncas dodged the blade. For a few terribly suspenseful moments, the two Indians—one good, one evil—

squared off, each staring into the other's war-painted face. Both were breathing hard, their bronzed, muscular bodies glistening with sweat. Hawkeye knew Uncas was the quickest fighter in the land. For some reason, though, the Mohican was not moving in for the kill.

Perhaps he has lost the will to live, Hawkeye thought with drooping ears. *After all, now his beloved Cora is gone.*

"Uncas, do not give up!" Hawkeye called out as loudly as he could.

With a deadly slowness, Magua stepped forward and thrust his knife straight into the Mohican's heart, just below the turtle tattoo. Even with the knife stuck deep in his chest, Uncas kept staring at Magua, stabbing the Huron with a glare of hate. Then the knees of Uncas buckled, and his youthful body fell across the lovely form of Cora.

Hawkeye closed his eyes with grief. He knew his dear Mohican friend had left this earthly world.

When the scout opened his eyes, he saw Magua leap off the rocky ledge and sail amazingly far through the air. He landed on another rocky ledge some distance below Hawkeye.

Now I have a clear shot at him, Hawkeye thought, as he fixed the rifle on Magua's body. *Magua thinks he just jumped out of my rifle's range, but this weapon reaches farther than he knows.*

Magua stared up at Hawkeye. An expression of hatred twisted like a snake across his face. He screamed out, "Listen to me, Hawkeye. Your people have begun to let the blood flow. But I shall finish it. Now I flee.

But one day I shall return to kill you . . . and Chingachgook . . . and anyone who displeases the eye of Magua!"

I do not want to shoot this man, Hawkeye thought, as he closed one eye to improve his aim. *This past week, I've seen enough fighting to last me a lifetime. I'm sickened by it. But I've let Magua get away twice, and dear friends of mine have paid for it with their blood. He cannot be allowed to escape again. So help me, I hope this is the very last time I am forced to shoot a fellow human.*

Hands raised to the dark clouds, Magua released a savage cry of victory.

With a steady paw, Hawkeye pulled back his rifle's trigger. As flame shot from the barrel, a splotch of dark red showed on Magua's side. The shot had been true. Magua staggered backward, clutching his chest. Then he toppled off the rocky ledge, yelling as he plunged to his death.

Hawkeye dropped his rifle with disgust.

Chapter Fifteen

Hawkeye gazed down into the graves of Cora and Uncas. He was attending their funeral in a patch of forest just outside the Delaware village. Many Delaware warriors had also been killed in the day's battle. The past few hours had been spent burying them. As the red, orange, and yellow shades of sunset bathed the woods in a wondrous glow, Hawkeye wiped away a tear with his paw.

The dead bodies of Cora and Uncas lay in birch containers that were carved to look like canoes. That was the traditional Indian way to bury the dead. They both had their eyes shut, as if they were peacefully asleep. Several young Delaware women stepped forward. They sprinkled scented herbs and fragrant wildflowers over the bodies.

All of the Delaware village had gathered. Duncan, Alice, David, and Uncas's father, Chingachgook, were also present. Even an officer of the French army was present. He had come to deliver a military message to the Hurons, and had ended up staying for the funeral ceremonies.

The aged chief, Tamenund, approached the bodies, assisted by the young boy. As the breeze gently tossed the Delaware's long snowy hair, he lifted his face to the sky. He spoke, his raspy voice weighted by sorrow. "Today the face of the Great Spirit is behind the clouds. We know not why He has taken these two, but we know He had good reason. We shall miss Uncas, he who could run with the leap of a deer. We shall miss Cora, she whose beauty matched that of the moon.

"Yesterday, I saw this man and woman look at each other and I could see there was love between their souls. Perhaps it is right that they have fallen together. Even now, the Great Spirit may be watching them walk hand in hand through that vast hunting ground in the sky."

Tamenund made a sign of blessing over the bodies.

The young Delaware women began a chant in honor of the dead. Their voices floated out a delicate melody.

Chingachgook stood motionless as stone, his eyes fixed on his son. Duncan, Alice, and David knelt beside the graves.

With tears streaming down her cheeks, Alice blew a kiss at Cora. Then she whispered, "Good-bye, dearest sister."

When the chant ended, several Delaware warriors stepped forward. They began to toss dirt and leafy plants over the bodies.

Hawkeye touched David with his paw and said, "David Gamut, perhaps you could send the two off with a pretty-sounding psalm."

"I don't think I shall," David said in a hollow voice. "I lost my pitch pipe somewhere. Besides, perhaps I should forget my singing and learn to become a fighter, instead. I have seen the necessity of battle in this land."

Hawkeye stuck his muzzle in his pouch and pulled out David's silver pitch pipe with his teeth. He dropped it on the ground and said, "After the battle, I found this shiny instrument lying in the dirt. I believe it belongs to you. You've proven yourself a decent fighter, but I think singing is your real gift."

David picked up the pitch pipe. "I thought I had lost this precious pitch pipe forever."

Hawkeye dug at the ground with his paw, considering something. "David, I've been thinking about our discussion the other night. You and Duncan and the sisters are good, civilized folks. Perhaps a little white civilization isn't such a bad thing. I just hope the white settlers don't start to chop down every tree in sight to put up their towns and cities."

David adjusted his spectacles. "I suppose civilization and nature must learn to live with each other in harmony."

"Well said," Hawkeye admitted.

David placed the pitch pipe to his lips and blew a musical tone. Then his mouth opened to sing a psalm of mourning.

Soon Chingachgook began to rock his body and chant an Indian hymn to his dead son. The Mohican's deep voice blended beautifully with David's smooth tenor, and all the forest seemed to drink in the music.

Hawkeye helped the Delawares cover the graves. By the time David and Chingachgook finished their songs, the bodies of Cora and Uncas were completely covered over.

As the sunset deepened into rich shades of purple and blue, the Delawares returned to their village. Duncan, Alice, and David knelt beside Hawkeye.

"We need to be on our way," Duncan said with sadness. "This French officer has agreed to supply us with horses. He knows the area well and has promised to escort us much of the way to Fort Edward."

Tough as he was, Hawkeye felt a pain in his heart, knowing it was time for good-byes.

"Brave scout, thank you," Alice said, wrapping her arms around Hawkeye's body. "You've saved my life so many times, I have begun to lose count."

"It's been a pleasure," Hawkeye said, enjoying the

female's soft touch. "There is no one who weeps or screams or faints with as much beauty as yourself."

"Farewell," David Gamut said, giving Hawkeye a scratch between the ears. "I have learned much from you, and perhaps you have learned a thing or two from me."

"Indeed, I have," Hawkeye said with a friendly wink.

Major Duncan Heyward looked about as close to tears as possible for an officer in the British army. "Sir, I do hope that you and I shall meet again someday."

Hawkeye gave Duncan's hand a fond shake with his paw. "This is a mighty big country, Major. They say it rolls on toward the west for thousands of miles. No one even knows exactly how far. Its history hasn't even been written yet. But if you find yourself traveling where there are beautiful woods and roaming animals and streams with crystal-clear waters, there's a good chance you'll cross the path of Hawkeye."

The three travelers said their good-byes to Chingachgook. Then Hawkeye watched Duncan, Alice, and David disappear into the forest in the company of the French officer.

This was a memorable event, Hawkeye thought, as he rested his furred belly against the earth. *British, French, and Indians all mourning side by side. And then there's me, an American. Too bad it took a tragedy to bring us all together in peace.*

Now Hawkeye and Chingachgook were the only ones left by the graves. The scout felt the need to say a final farewell to his friend Uncas. He tilted his muzzle upward and released a howl so full of sadness that it could have made a wolf weep.

Chingachgook knelt down and placed a firm hand on Hawkeye's furred neck. "My brother," he said in his native language, "do not sorrow too much. The Great Spirit had need for my boy, Uncas, and his many gifts. So He called him away. Long ago, the Great Spirit also had need for my wife, the mother of Uncas. It is meant to be. And, finally, the Great Spirit has meant for me to be alone."

"No, you are not alone," Hawkeye said, rubbing his muzzle against Chingachgook's arm. "You and I may be of a different color, but the Great Spirit has arranged for us to journey along the same path. No matter where you go, your friend Hawkeye will always be nearby."

As Chingachgook kept his hand on Hawkeye, the two men shed many tears to water the graves of Uncas and Cora. Soon Hawkeye noticed Tamenund standing on the other side of the graves, supported by the young boy. Behind him stood the darkening shapes of countless trees.

The aged chief spoke in a voice that sounded very much like the sighing of the wind. "The sunset falls on the forest, throwing darkness over all living things that dwell here. I am glad for this. Of all my many days, this has been the longest. For on this day, I have lived to see the death of a brave warrior. He is a young man who, aside from his father, is the last of the noble race of the Mohicans."

As the sunlight vanished, the leaves whispered a final blessing over the graves.

I had forgotten how sad the ending of this story is. Let me just take a moment . . .

Okay, let's get back to the other story. Fortunately, it has a much happier ending.

Chapter Sixteen

Wishbone lay in the rich green grass of Jackson Park. Joe, Sam, David, and Mr. Bloodgood sat on the ground nearby. After finishing their dinner at home, the kids and Wishbone had gone to the park to meet with Mr. Bloodgood. The lush colors of a summer sunset painted the sky, and Wishbone could hear the crickets begin their night song.

"I still don't know how Wishbone managed to find that torn page," Joe said, looking at Wishbone with a puzzled expression on his face.

"I've explained it to you several times," Wishbone told Joe. "Why is it that no one ever listens to the dog? Huh? Tell me that, would you, please?"

Mr. Bloodgood met Wishbone's eyes. "My ancestors believed in something called 'shape shifting.' That's when a human changes himself into some type of animal. Maybe it also works in reverse. Maybe Wishbone somehow changed himself into a human. Or maybe he's just one very intelligent dog."

Wishbone gave Mr. Bloodgood a fond look. "Thank you for understanding, sir."

"However it happened," Sam said, sweeping her hand through the grass, "everything worked out for the best. Now there will be no Tastee Oasis in our beautiful park."

"Not for now, at least," Mr. Bloodgood added. "But I have a feeling Mr. King will make another attempt to build his Tastee Oasis somewhere around here. It's a story that's been going on for centuries, and I doubt it will end anytime soon."

"If Mr. King tries to build near here again," David said boldly, "we'll fight him again."

"You know what I would like to do now?" Mr. Bloodgood said as he stood up. "I'd like to perform a Native American ceremony of thanks. Would all of you join me?"

"We'd love to!" Sam exclaimed, as Wishbone and all three kids sprang to their feet.

154

"Let's see," Mr. Bloodgood said, pulling a dog biscuit from his pocket. "I need something to use as an offering. The only thing I have is a leftover dog treat. I suppose that'll work. Wishbone, do you promise not to eat this?"

"Uh . . . well . . ." Wishbone said, licking his chops. "If it's being used for a good cause, I suppose I can control myself."

After getting the group to form a circle, Mr. Bloodgood lifted the dog biscuit to the sky. "Great Spirit, our Father," he said, filling each word with meaning, "we thank You for everything that You have created."

Mr. Bloodgood touched the biscuit to the earth.

"Beautiful earth, our mother, we thank you for sharing this wonderful planet with us. And today we especially thank you for allowing us to have this park. Right here we may find and enjoy all of your elements— the fire of the sun, the waters of the duck pond, the wind that blows through the trees, and the earth of the ground."

Wishbone felt a slight breeze caress his fur, and he heard a gentle rustling in the leaves.

As Mr. Bloodgood continued, he held the biscuit in each of the four directions. "Wabun, spirit-keeper of the east . . . Waboose, spirit-keeper of the north . . . Shawnodese, spirit-keeper of the south . . . And Mudje-keewis, spirit-keeper of the west . . . We thank you for the four seasons and all the great many gifts you bring our way."

Wishbone noticed two squirrels watching the ceremony from the limb of a tree. *You know, it almost looks like they're listening,* Wishbone thought. *But that can't be. Squirrels aren't that intelligent . . . are they?*

Mr. Bloodgood knelt and dug up some earth with his hands. Wishbone stepped over to lend a paw. When Mr. Bloodgood set the biscuit in the hole, Wishbone covered it over with dirt. Then Mr. Bloodgood rocked back and forth a few moments, chanting softly to himself. When he finished the chant, Mr. Bloodgood stood. "Well, that completes the ceremony, folks."

"That was beautiful," Sam said in an awed voice.

"And very cool," David added.

"Do you think those spirits really heard you?" Joe asked as he glanced around the park.

Mr. Bloodgood smiled as his long hair blew in the breeze. "Oh, it's hard to say for sure. But I like to believe they did. Listen, do you hear the trees rustling? I think they're telling us the spirits are pleased with our prayer."

Wishbone raised his ears. "You know, I think you're right. I think that's exactly what they're telling us."

Mr. Bloodgood reached down to pat Wishbone's back, as if he understood what the dog had just said.

Everyone stood there for a moment, enjoying the quiet peace of the park. The soft beams of twilight filtered through the trees, giving them an almost magical appearance.

"I guess we should get home," Joe said finally. "It's hard to leave, though. It's so nice here right now."

"Well, look at the bright side," Wishbone said, his

tail wagging with contentment. "We can come back tomorrow and the next day and the day after that. I feel certain this park will stay the way it is for many years to come. Especially if we keep sharing our dog treats with the Great Spirit!"

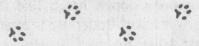

Hoot! It was quite a day, wasn't it? Like Hawkeye, I feel as if I've traveled many long miles and fought many hard battles. I've also learned to appreciate the nature around me even more deeply than I did before. And there is no better book for helping one really get in touch with the earth than *The Last of the Mohicans!*

About James Fenimore Cooper

James Fenimore Cooper, much like the character Hawkeye, was a pathfinder. He is often considered to be the first American novelist. He wasn't the first American to write a novel, but he was the first to make a steady living by writing. More important, he was the first novelist to portray the history, landscape, and spirit of North America.

Born in 1798 to a wealthy family, Cooper grew up in the woods of New York State. He entered college at the age of thirteen, but he was expelled for pulling such pranks as placing a donkey in a professor's chair! After that, he went to sea for a while. Later, he married.

When his family lost its fortune, Cooper needed a new source of income. After reading a romantic English novel, he claimed he could write a similar type of book himself. His wife dared him to do it, and he did.

However, Cooper's next novel, *The Spy*, was something entirely different. It was an adventure set during the American Revolution. Unlike the first book, this one sold quite well.

In 1826, Cooper published *The Last of the Mohicans*, which became a major success both in the United States and overseas. The book's main character, Hawkeye, had been featured in one of Cooper's earlier novels, and the author also used him in three following novels. These five books—*The Pioneers, The Last of the Mohicans,*

The Prairie, *The Pathfinder*, and *The Deerslayer*—are often known collectively as the Leather-Stocking Tales, because Hawkeye is called by that name in one of the stories. The tough, almost mythic Hawkeye was a truly American creation, and Cooper's books about him were what first put the United States on the map of world literature. In addition to supplying plenty of thrills and excitement, these stories showed how America changed from a wilderness to a largely civilized land.

Cooper wrote more than fifty books, including travel essays, historical studies, and sea adventures, a type of tale that he invented. And, like a true pioneer, he kept on writing until his death, in 1851.

About *The Last of the Mohicans*

*T*he *Last of the Mohicans* is what is known as a historical novel. Though it is a make-believe story, it takes place against a background of real history—in this case, the French and Indian War. The historical novel was invented by the Scottish writer Sir Walter Scott, the author of *Ivanhoe*. James Fenimore Cooper is sometimes known as the "American Scott."

There is at least one historical fact with which Cooper took liberty. Chingachgook and Uncas were not really "the last of the Mohicans." In 1757, there were still several hundred living members of the Mohican tribe. The Mohicans went on to fight bravely alongside the American colonists in the Revolutionary War. Today, however, there are no pure-blooded Mohicans remaining.

Though made up, Hawkeye is one of the most memorable characters in all literature. Cooper allowed the scout to star in five different books. Hawkeye, the heroic man who lives apart from civilization, has been much imitated over the years. For example, he was the forerunner of the Lone Ranger, Indiana Jones, and just about every character that movie star John Wayne ever played. The five books featuring Hawkeye also inspired the type of rugged adventure that came to be known as the "western" or "frontier" story.

The Last of the Mohicans is also known for its excellent portrayal of the New York State wilderness.

Cooper wished to capture the area's natural beauty in words so there would be a record of it after much of it had been cut away by civilization. Around this same time, a group of painters known as the Hudson River School attempted to do the same thing with their landscape paintings of the area. Indeed, today most of that wilderness has been replaced by cities and towns.

The Last of the Mohicans was very popular in its day, and it has since become one of the world's most famous novels. Most everyone has heard of the title, and the story has been made into at least five movie versions. Although much of their beloved wilderness has disappeared, Hawkeye and his Mohican friends are certain to live forever.

About Alexander Steele

Alexander Steele is a writer of books, plays, and screenplays for both juveniles and adults . . . and sometimes for dogs. *The Last of the Breed* is his second book for The Adventures of Wishbone series, his first being *Moby Dog*. He has also written *Tale of the Missing Mascot*, *Case of the On-Line Alien*, and *Case of the Unsolved Case* for the WISHBONE Mysteries series.

Mystery and history are favorite subjects for Alexander. He has written ten detective novels for juveniles. He is now at work on a novel for adults that deals with the beginning of detectives in both fiction and real life. Among Alexander's plays is the award-winning *One Glorious Afternoon*, which features Shakespeare and his fellow players at the Globe Theatre.

As a youngster, Alexander loved movie westerns. When he finally read James Fenimore Cooper's *The Last of the Mohicans*, he understood the source and inspiration of all those great movies. All the elements were in the book—the loner hero, the noble Indians, the mean Indians, the damsels in distress, and, of course, the heart-pounding chase scenes. While preparing this book, Alexander reread *The Last of the Mohicans*; he also read *The Deerslayer*, a story that features Hawkeye as a young man. For the young reader who likes excitement, Alexander recommends trying to hike with Hawkeye through the pages of these books!

Alexander lives in New York City, where Native Americans were the very first inhabitants.

Coming Soon!

#17
The Adventures of
WISHBONE™
DIGGING TO THE CENTER OF THE EARTH
By Michael Anthony Steele
Inspired by A Journey to the Center of the Earth
by Jules Verne
The Adventures of WISHBONE
#17
DIGGING TO THE CENTER OF THE EARTH

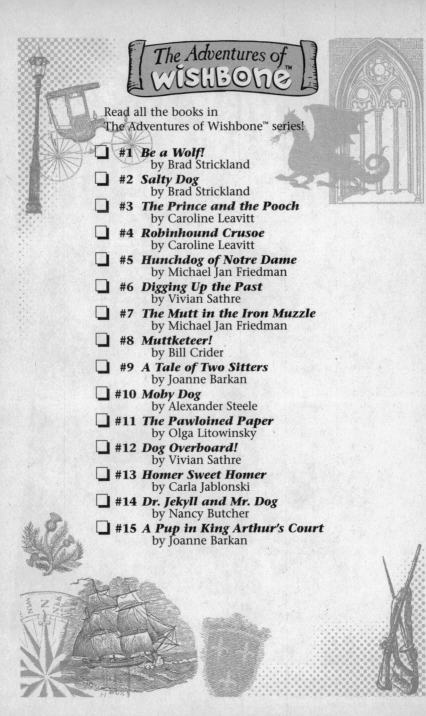

The Adventures of WISHBONE™

Read all the books in
The Adventures of Wishbone™ series!

WISHBONE Mysteries

Read all the books in the
WISHBONE™ Mysteries series!

WHAT HAS FOUR LEGS, A HEALTHY COAT, AND A GREAT DEAL ON MEMBERSHIP?

IT'S THE WISHBONE™ ZONE
THE OFFICIAL WISHBONE FAN CLUB!

When you enter the **WISHBONE ZONE,** you get:
- Color poster of **Wishbone**™
- A one-year subscription to *The WISHBONE ZONE News*– that's at least four issues of the hottest newsletter around!
- Autographed photo of **Wishbone** and his friends
- **WISHBONE** sunglasses, and more!

To join the fan club, pay $10 and charge your **WISHBONE ZONE** membership to VISA, MasterCard, or Discover. Call:

1-800-888-WISH

Or send us your name, address, phone number, birth date, and a check for $10 payable to Big Feats! (TX residents add $.83 sales tax). Write to:

WISHBONE ZONE
P.O. Box 9523
Allen, TX 75013-9523

Prices and offer are subject to change. Place your order now!